LITTLE GIRL BEAUTIFUL

Walter W Mason

CONTENTS

CHAPTER 1

Sebastian's angular features showed no expression. He cried when the man pushed him toward the cliff edge. He cried and tried to cover his eyes as he watched the rape of his little brother. His crying stopped when he heard neck bones snap with a dull crack and he knew Anthony was gone forever He held the short branch in his hand, it felt heavy.

The day they disappeared was a ragged Sunday. Oppressive Heat and a plague of stinging, itching insects shortened tempers and raised stress levels. Clouds thickened and boiled over the mountaintop.

Serifano cursed and kicked at the thick dust in front of his farm shed.

"There is no worry," he said with a gruff voice.

"They're hiding inside the cane for sure but when they come out, then I'll teach them properly."

He slapped the broad blade of the cane knife against his leg and kicked again at the imprint of a tractor tyre in the dust.

"I'll teach them not to hide from their father."

The old woman standing with him spoke in Italian, her gaze on the mountain range.

"They are only boys Serifano. My grandsons, you know I'm old and when you grow old you will understand that life no longer holds dreams, just tears and memories. Go and find them, leave your weapon at home and show them you love them."

Seated in the shade of an old Bloodwood tree the two boys spoke softly. The older boy was apprehensive, the younger, excited. Simmo was going to show them the wallabies jumping over the waterfall.

"You sure this is the way," the small boy asked, "remember what Mr Jack said when he was gonna take us at Easter? Across the grid in the fenced paddock then up the green ridge. He told us."

The other boy shook his head and looked at the rainforest that bordered the green ridge. A man approached wearing a dirty yellow shirt, a battered yellow hat held in one hand, rubbing his crutch with the other.

"What's he been doin' in the bush?" The small boy asked.

"Dunno, he's queer, old Simmo."

The small boy nodded.

"Come on," the man shouted, "if we don't get a move on, we won't see them wallabies jumpin' over the falls".

The track became steeper as they climbed. When the steep gradient stopped any possibility of wheeled traffic, Simmo led them into the rainforest. For fifteen minutes they struggled up a steep embankment. When they reached level ground the thick trees ended unnaturally. The boys surged ahead.

"Stop!" Simmo shouted. "You been taught better than that. Look at the bloody stinging tree. You're gonna barge into that."

The boys stopped, within touching distance, grew a ragged line of plants, some impressive in their spread, others still fighting to establish themselves.

The boy's father impressed on them the agony caused by the caress of the stinging tree. He told them to touch the heart-shaped leaves just once. The excruciating pain they felt was the accepted way to teach kids how to recognise the plant, they drew back.

"Good. Simmo nodded and led them through a thicket of feral lantana onto a natural terrace.

"See this place. You're on sacred ground now. Abos got a story about a Dreamtime giant who used to live here. That giant Left footprints like this on the mountain."

The boys showed no interest in the story as they slowly walked through the flat area with strange weeds growing taller than they were, intermingled with Casuarina trees.

The older boy grabbed a handful of the jagged-shaped leaves, rubbed them between his hands and held them to his nose.

The man watched, "makes you excited doin' that." He copied the boy's actions.

"This is a sacred place for your old man as well." He chuckled. "This is what buys him his new tractors and flash cars". He herded the boys on. As they left the giant's footprint he looked back. Today I'll get me reward. Keep your mouth shut Simmo. Mention the footprint and I'll cut your balls off Simmo. Well, today I'll get it all, then we'll take the trip, and they'll know old Simmo taught them a lesson. He used his yellow hat to wipe the sweat from his face.

The night was coming. The waterfall's roar faded in and out as it echoed in the deep gorge. From his cramped position in the Lantana Sebastian could just see the top of the gorge where it sloped down to the edge. Simmo's yellow shirt was visible in the gloom. He wiped blood from his torn ear and winched when he touched his bruised cheek, still, he focused on the man where he squatted a dozen steps from the edge. More than a thousand feet straight down into the gorge, he'd been told. He held back a sob as the dying sun caught his little brother's face, now smeared with blood and slack in death.

"Won't be long now Anthony," crooned Simmo, "soon as we find your brother we can all take the trip together."

The waterfall roared. The night was close. The rain came down. Sebastian knew what he was going to do.

Simmo stood up, still holding the body. Sebastian crawled from the lantana, walked quietly up behind the man and swung the branch. Simmo staggered, with a surge Sebastian shoved him over the precipice still clutching Anthony's body.

He didn't go close enough to watch the murderer fall. The scream tod him what he wanted to know.

Serifano was frantic. He drove the old tractor across the cattle grid, hand-held floodlight swinging and bouncing. Even above his tractor's engine noise, he could hear the neighbour's Toyota Land Cruiser screaming as it ploughed through the mud that was their property's dividing headland. "Christ, when this is over', I'll have a month's work fixing their bloody roads he muttered. 'When I find them fuckin' kids I'll give 'em a shovel each and they can do the job".

The rain sheeted down. Water roared through Silverload Creek to the right and Waterfall Creek in the gorge further away to the left. As he fought wrist-snapping jerks of the steering wheel, he whistled 'The Lion Sleeps Tonight'.

Five kilometres from where the tractor shuddered and slewed as it crawled up the green ridge, Serafino's brother stood with three men on the high bank of Waterfall Creek where it boiled and foamed out of the gorge. They could see silhouettes like an advancing horde of giants brought to life in the brilliance of two aircraft landing lights fitted to Serifano's tractor.

"He's doin' it." Dublin Jack said in a matter-of-fact tone.

"What did you expect? He's got a head like a rock." Giuseppe (Joe) Castorana reached through the rain to another of the searchers. "Rosario! Get back to the shed, get the new Chamberlain and follow him to the first saddle in the ridge. But no further understand. It's too steep after that and the tractor will flip over backwards".

Rosario turned; a sullen boy of fourteen, he resented every instruction he received. In the dull light from the State Emergency Service Land Cruiser, his petulance was apparent.

"Why the hell take a tractor? What's wrong with the Toyota? At least I'd be dry in that, and it won't cartwheel down the hill. You're in charge Mr. Jack. Tell him the Toyota's best."

"Yep! And I'm tellin' you Ross. You do what your father says." He watched as the boy trudged through a break in the cane. "Bloody kids! I was flat out keepin' young Tully at home tonight. Wanted to come out and look for his mates."

The fourth man spoke as the rain dripped from his broad nose, "You're right there boss. I had to tell Albert some old Murri legends about monsters around the Castorana farm to get the little midget to stay home."

Dublin jerked off his sodden hat and wrung the water out. "You mob got a legend for everything. And, if you think about it, they all mean something."

"No sense in a legend if it doesn't mean something."

"Never mind about Aboriginal legends," Joe Castorana looked at the old house visible on the vast flat area of She-oak Ridge, "That farm's got spooks alright. Even the Black Hand stand-over men disappeared when they came around here."

"All right! Let's get the spotlights and do what we need to do." Dublin climbed into the Land Cruiser and drove as near as he dared to the edge of the high bank of Waterfall Creek.

The tractor's slow progress stopped altogether. Serifano cursed and kicked the diff-lock on. The front wheels lifted off the ground. He shoved the clutch pedal home, and the front crashed back to the ground. With a shrug, he resumed whistling, locked the brakes on and scanned the ridge ahead with the floodlight. Suddenly he leaned forward. Huddled under a bloodwood tree off to the side of the ridge he saw Sebastian. Fear shot through him; he couldn't see his youngest son "Where's Tony?" Serifano shouted down the beam of the floodlight.

The boy only grasped his legs tighter to his chest.

Serifano kicked off the break lock. Eyes still on his son as he shoved the throttle lever down and released the clutch. With a shudder, the tractor spun deeper into the mud then under full power it lifted from the front, pivoting on rear wheels, it whipped over centre and crashed upside-down.

Sebastian ran to his father, he tried but could do nothing; Serifano was pinned with no chance of escape, the tractor wheels still spinning. He watched as his father died.

Joe Castorana held the spotlight on an object that spun and tumbled in the floodwater. The three men watched without words for the few seconds it took the thing to swirl out of view. During that short time, a smudge of yellow appeared and disappeared as the object rolled. They looked at each other.

CHAPTER 2

Each of us sat for a time with his own thoughts. Drawn by the campfire, my memories wandered over the past day, and then further through the years that shaped our lives. Lyn absently prodded the fire; his face reflected the contented mood that fell easily over our camp. Wavering firelight matched the rhythm of nearby Silverload Creek as it shouldered a path to its destination. Forever changing, forever remaining the same.

Four men dedicated to the God that is saltwater, who thrive on bleaching, burning sun and busting big fish. Quietly we sit relaxed and happy beside the freshwater only a couple of kilometres from where it escapes from the mountain. No aching shoulders. No strained body and mind from endless hours of trolling for game fish in jarring seas. Today the longest drag-burning fish run was five metres, not enough to bring a brief smoulder to the little Abu fishing reel. The shouts of excitement generated by that fish's run were something to hear and giving the jungle perch back its freedom was a more personal thing than saltwater anglers know.

"Tomorrow I'll go feed that flagtail." Until now Lyn had no idea freshwater held anything but Barramundi. At times he even dismissed that legendary fighter as overrated.

"Feed a Jungle perch?" someone asked. "What's your game? You want to fatten it up for next year?"

Lyn was upset his motives were being questioned and somehow needed to explain why he felt as he did after his encounter with the tough little fish. "That fish deserves a free meal. I upset his life for my own excitement. I pay my debts."

We understood his thinking.

"I'll tell you mate." Busty was moved enough to put together a sentence or two. We waited, silent and expectant, to hear what came next. "Tomorrow, I'll help you feed that fish, and I'll leave my rod in camp."

What a mental picture that was. Fit all 125 kg of Busty into a suit topped with a small hat and you'd call him Godfather. The last time I heard emotion in his voice was when he landed a 400kg Marlin and then all he said was Mate that fish could pull a bit. Now he was going without weapons to feed a fish that might never grow to more than 3kg.

"Well, if you two are going to feed that little flagtail. I'll throw a couple of yabbies to the blackie at the other end of the pool." Al had cast for almost an hour at a clearly visible Sooty Grunter just before sunset. The fish followed every cast right to Al's shadow then turned and took up its original station across the pool. In the end, Al was playing games with the Sooty. He would halt his retrieve; and allow the current to swing his lure downstream into the bank. The fish wasn't fooled. It would then ignore the lure and swim straight to where Al's shadow fell onto the water before retreating to its home across the pool. "That is if no one wants to eat it". He added, looking at me.

I was feeling left out. Rather than play with fish or make plans to feed them I caught and kept mine. They were the meal we enjoyed less than half an hour ago. Now I felt as though I'd eaten an old friend of the family. "For years I've tried to tell you there's nothing like a few days on the sweet water," I said, moving the subject from the consumption of personal friends. "And this is the best stream I've ever seen. Unfortunately, the landowner is hard to get on with."

Busty grunted. He is the landowner and every time I fish the Silverload, we go through the same routine. I knock at his front door, which is always answered by one of his four young daughters. I ask if I may speak to Sebastian. The girl always shouts out to her father saying it's his old school friend. The one he always talks about football with. The other kids hide around doorways or behind coffee tables and peer at me as though I've come to steal their toys.

Busty comes to the door "Yeah?" he asks with a deep frown.

We grew up together. Played football and toured the country together. Had our moments together and tried hard to forget some of them. Now I find him looking at me as if I really had come to steal the kid's toys. I ask if, during the coming weekend, I might go onto his property and fish the creek. His answer is always the same. I can fish the creek if I don't shoot the cattle, start a fire in the cane or climb the green ridge.

It's a long time since I shot anything, I'm careful with fires and it's a tough climb up the green ridge to the waterfall so I assure him, all will be left as I find it. Permission is granted and we generally have a beer.

The others smile. Busty has a fierce reputation and they have always been happy for me to act as a buffer.

Albert Harold Harvey, Al to his friends and Mr. Harvey or A H to the rest, is a renowned Aboriginal filmmaker specialising in creatures that bite, sting, scratch or poison in obscure and painful ways. His favourite is the Queensland crocodile. Al's eyes normally have a glazed look from shuttling between continents and, I think, making money. It's been years since he actually looked into a crock's mouth or focused a camera on a Queensland stinging tree.

Now Al is relaxed, grinning that evil grin we were used to seeing just before he committed some act of thuggery on the football field.

"If it isn't black Mr. Harvey, back from the dead," I said as seriously as I could. "Bit of relaxation's welcome news to your brain mate."

"No racist remarks in this camp." Growled Lyn, "We've got a Murri and a Wog who both know, in police speak, how to defend themselves."

Busty and Al both laughed, and Al followed up, "Well you're no Murri, Wog or mix are you mate? Just pure bloody arsehole."

Lyndon Smith is a police senior sergeant, a job that seems to lever aside his good nature and replace it with a frown. He tells us he teaches people how to live a good life. He owns a nice game fishing boat inherited from his father, one of the biggest farmers in the district, which he uses as often as possible. Still, he went away to school, as did his father. Because of that, he is not considered a true local.

Busty scowled, and then laughed, "Tomorrow Roxanne and the girls come for the day. Then we'll have an army of Wogs and you rough and tough Poms, Murries, Irishmen or whatever won't say a single bloody word out of place because you know you'll get eaten."

I awoke the next morning to the sound of Richard Harris blasting out Macarthur Park. Busty stood in front of his tent looking down at the long pool and laughing. Beside the water, Lyn struggled with what was certainly an extra-large eel. Above on the granite boulders Al sat beside a CD player conducting game-boat procedure. Each of us had his fighting music and Lyn's was vibrating around the gorge before breakfast.

The bend in Lyn's rod proved his absolute faith in the rod builder who happened to be Busty. The man performed miracles with thread and fibreglass and just as well in this case.

As Lyn slid the bad-tempered length of teeth and muscle onto the rocks Al wound down the volume, jumped down and covered the eel with an old towel. With the end of the music came the labouring pitch of a diesel engine.

"Quick!" Busty shouted. "Make more breakfast! Here comes Rocky."

After breakfast there was a general, it's time to do stuff movement. I searched the faces and asked who was going to help polish the camp. Busty set off with his four daughters to explore the top pool. Lyn had important activities to undertake up at the next pool. Al took breakfast leftovers to feed his new fish friend in the long pool.

"Just you and me," I said to Roxanne.

"In your dreams Town." In high school she'd decided, because she thought I'd been named after a town, she'd call me Town. My objections failed and she often did.

As I finished clearing up, I could hear her talking and laughing with Al. I felt a brief pang of jealousy, so I grabbed my fishing gear and went to the next pool downstream. I sat in contemplation for a couple of hours with no thought of catching fish until a stone hit the water close by. I waited without turning.

"You're not catching anything," Roxanne said.

"Caught you, didn't I?"

"Mongrel in every way." She said.

"OK tell me why."

She threw another stone, closer this time. "Tully why do you always try to make me angry?"

I used my most charming smile. "It must be because I love you Rocky." I had to duck the next stone.

"Now I'm even angrier and I'm going to tell Busty what you just said."

"OK! OK! Doll. I'm sorry for joking."

"Joking?' Now she looked really upset. 'Well don't joke."

I shrugged. It was time to give up.

"Why don't you come to see us anymore? I don't mean to have a quick beer with Busty. I mean all of us. The girls, me and Busty." She sat beside me. "I'm serious Tully".

I waited until her frown left. "It's true Rocky. I do love you. I love you all, but you're a family, you're all there together. I'd just be hanging around with nothing to contribute."

She held my arm with both hands, "Of course you've got something to add, and I want to see you. We all want to see you. Even if we just go out together. You and your latest woman."

She was my first love, my first lover. For her, I guessed it was a simple memory. For me, even though I couldn't recognise it at the time, it should have been the beginning of my life. Instead, I had to head for the bright lights. A big city crime reporter, a famous journalist with contacts throughout the nation. I hid the country boy. I never mentioned a father with a string of community service awards who fought fires and rescued flood victims. I exorcised, with the help of hard work and brash city girls, the green-eyed farmer's daughter who fought to hold her place in my heart.

They were thoughts I could never voice. She stood slowly and walked to the pool's far end.

Half an hour later Al's voice broke the silence. "Roxanne! You got your phone? Busty's trying to call you."

"Why?"

"He wants to know why you kept Stella down here."

"What's he talking about? Stella's not here none of the kids have been here."

"Well, he said he sent Bobby and Stella down here to bring up the yabbie net hours ago."

She frowned, "what's he doing sending little girls on his errands? Let me use your phone." She stabbed at the phone with her finger until she was satisfied with the number, then held it to her ear with an impatient frown. I moved closer waiting to hear a Rocky explosion. I had sympathy for Busty and what he was about to cop.

"Trust him to wander around out of range." She thrust the phone in Al's direction.

I volunteered to go up to the top pool and find out what was happening. In the end, we all started the climb collecting Lyn at the next pool.

Silverload Creek was a series of pools torn into the bedrock. Huge granite boulders made clambering from pool to pool almost impossible unless the climber knew the ancient path. Al led us unerringly, each step replicating those first made thousands of years ago and taught to him by his father.

I tried to help Roxanne through the first hard section. She slapped my hand away saying she didn't need me dragging her over the rocks, I only made it more difficult.

The way Busty took his daughters up to the top pool was an easy thirty-five-minute climb from our campsite up the green ridge. From there, a five-minute scramble down the old track to the water would have caused more girlish excitement than complaint. Our journey up through the creek cut ten minutes off that time.

Al stopped as we came to the bottom end of the pool, "I've never said anything before, but this pool has meaning for my mob, you know, it's called the birthing pool, that's because the women would come here to have their babies. The banks are smooth rock and in places, you can step straight into the water. Over the other side of the pool before it falls into the valley there's a small spring in a flat area. That's the fertility spring. The women who wanted to get pregnant would spend a night there drinking the spring water." He grinned, "It wasn't a popular place for the girls, and they avoided it like the plague."

Rocky shook her head, "I love to hear your stories Al, they bring the country to life. Luckily I didn't go near that spring, or I might have ten kids."

Al smiled and pointed to the other end of the pool.

Splashes and shouts of delight showed Busty's lack of concern over his missing daughter.

"Bloody fishing didn't last long," Al growled as we watched a rain of little girls hitting the water close to Busty. He stood, waist-deep in the water and gathered them in until he had an armful of laughing, struggling, bodies.

Pushing between Al and me, Roxanne ended the fun with a glare at her husband and a brief command to the girls, "Out. Dressed and sit." She was obeyed without question.

Busty frowned as he stepped up onto the bank. "Where's Stella?"

I felt cold. My father's words inside my head. "That old farm, it takes people. It takes people and never gives them up."

Roxanne looked at him. I could see the fear in her face. "We haven't seen her Busty. What happened? Why did you send her down to us?"

He looked confused. Before he could answer, his oldest daughter, Bobby spoke. "It was her idea, Mummy. I didn't like fishing so she said we should go back and bring up the yabbie trap."

Busty broke in, "I said no but then she said she wanted to bring back some biscuits she helped you make last night."

Roxanne stood with hands on hips shaking her head. Bobby resumed the story. "Daddy took us up the slidy track and Stella said she knew the way. She'd walked right up the road and climbed up to the waterfall two times before." In the distance, the waterfall roared.

"Then where did she go?" Roxanne demanded of her daughter.

"I don't know Mummy. She just went down to the tiny creek to get some ferns for Tully, and she didn't come back."

They looked at me. I shrugged. I liked to grow ferns they all knew that. Stella, even at ten years old, was aware of what men liked and tried to earn their attention.

"What then Honey?" I asked Bobby gently.

"Nothing Tully. I knew she was hiding and trying to scare me, so I came back."

"Bobby!" Roxanne's tone was severe, her face harsh with worry.

"Come on Roxanne," Al interjected as he stroked Bobby's wet hair. "Stella probably just heard a noise and thought it was a wild pig or a Cassowary. I bet she's up a tree and too frightened to come down."

"I think she might have gone to the giant's footprint, "Busty said.

"Why?" Rocky demanded.

"Well, when I took her there, she liked the smell."

Rocky scowled.

"Your field of gold Sebastian".

He looked down and turned away from her.

"It's not my gold. Uncle Joe's and that prick Ross's gold. Nothing to do with us since Dad died"

"It's your land. You need to start saying no."

The giant's footprints had been used for Castorana's hidden marijuana crop for years starting with Giuseppe and Serafino's father. There was little danger of people stumbling on the crop as the footprint was almost inaccessible. The track, purposely hidden and little used, was through a thick screen of trees. Even Joe Castorana's crop sitters had their camp well hidden and were careful not to use the same track in and out.

Rocky pushed her husband. "Go and find her you stupid man. Hurry! I'm really worried."

Busty looked at Lynn.

"Come on mate. We'll go and find Stella." He looked in my direction. "Can you give Rocky a hand to pack the gear and take it back to the house? And Tully, please don't say a word to anyone. If searches come tramping around up here, they might find stuff that shouldn't be found."

I frowned said nothing.

He grabbed my shoulder. "Tully! I'm going to take care of it once and for all. I'll take care of it,"

CHAPTER 3

Al and I broke the camp and carried the gear up to Rocky's Land Cruiser.

With the girls safely aboard, she drove back to the farmhouse.

Al looked worried. "I want to tell you Tully God knows I need to tell you. You're Busty's best friend. He's closer to you than anyone else and I'm worried. If Stella is really gone, I don't think he will handle it." He picked up a rock and threw it, so it bounced off the granite boulders and into the water. "Shit mate! Remember when we were kids how he would go berserk if anyone threatened you or me or even Lynn and when Roxanne came into the picture, he was even worse."

I nodded. On more than one occasion Busty turned a racist remark directed at Al into a slaughter. If his ferocious punches weren't enough, he used head or feet or whatever he needed to leave no opponent standing.

"He's a tough bastard all right."

Al hit my shoulder. "It's more than that. You and I, we're tough bastards. We might go down but there'll be blood on the ground first. Not Busty. You couldn't pull him away. While there was a threat he wouldn't stop."

I wasn't happy to be reminded of my part in a few of these incidents and I'm sure Al felt the same.

"It's been years since that shit," I said.

Al shook his head. "It's still there. Fuck mate it's still there. A few months ago, he saw someone he thought was following Bobby at the circus. He had that creep by the throat in less than 10 seconds. If Rocky and I hadn't been there he'd be doing time now."

He cleared a patch of ground and drew aimlessly with a stick. I grabbed his arm.

"Where the hell are you taking me here Al?"

He looked at me. "Like I said. If something bad has happened to Stella, you need to watch him. You need to look after him."

Although no slouch when it came to walking, I found a lot to distract me as I walked back to the farmhouse. A big old echidna waddled across the track. When I approached too quickly it rolled into a spiny ball and waited for me to pass, when I stopped it started to bury itself. A picture of Busty in his late teens racing across a ploughed and harrowed cane paddock, came to mind. He was running to catch an echidna we'd seen as we were planting cane.

"If I don't move him the tractor will squash him." He shouted as he started after what looked like a cannonball full of prickles. He wore gloves, necessary for planting cane, so when he scooped the creature up, he was safe from the spines, He carried it over to the headland and released it into the grass.

"Should have kept the thing and put it into Cousin Ross' bed." We both laughed.

At that time Ross was already heading for a life in his father's shadow. Although he thought of himself as a standover man, he didn't dare stand over anyone but women and kids. He sometimes needled Busty; he would never go as far as to create a physical confrontation. Busty wouldn't back down and animosity had already developed between them.

I slowly walked around the echidna, resisting the urge to prod it with a stick as it buried itself. I kept walking, I couldn't delay any longer. Finally, my old blue Nissan Patrol farm ute came into sight. That vehicle got me out of more tough situations than I cared to think about. I climbed in, slammed the door and headed down the farm track with more than gentle wheel spin.

I couldn't understand how Stella would leave her older sister and go up to the footprint alone or even climb the last stretch to the waterfall alone. I began calculating the time. They must have been gone for more than two hours, more like two and a half. Walking down to where Rocky had parked would take fifteen minutes. Climbing back to their swimming hole probably thirty minutes. Rocky's vehicle was within our sight, yet we didn't see them going to it to get the biscuits.

By the time the track joined the headland of Busty's twenty-five-acre home paddock, I'd decided to skirt his house and drive straight to town. Somewhere during the twenty-minute drive, I'd lost the courage to broach Roxanne and ask the questions that I wanted to ask.

Busty came to see me that night. He didn't want Roxanne to know but he wanted me to go down to Sydney and question Joe. He needed to be certain his uncle's men had nothing to do with Stella's disappearance. He would join me when he could.

CHAPTER 4

Traffic roared and belched its way along George Street. Noxious fumes, obnoxious drivers and blasting horns sharply returned me to the horror of city life.

Joe Castorana, tall and surprisingly thin was always a man careful with money. He selected a small change purse from the two dozen on display. "She will like this one Tully. It is a very nice colour."

I nodded. "I think so Mr. Castorana. She likes bright colours."

He pursed his lips. "It is too expensive do you think?"

I shrugged. "You get what you pay for, and this one is five dollars. It isn't expensive."

"We bought this hotel. Serifano, me and our father. We bought it with nothing but the home farm behind us. When Serifano died because of that fucken twisted Simmo, I held Sebastian's share until he was a man. He told me to keep it. His business was farming. He could never see past the dirt. He still can't."

He paid for the purse, and we walked back into the street. "So, tell me why it is Tully that I'm talking to you and not my nephew, my family? Sebastian could not visit his old uncle?"

The situation was uncomfortable, but I'd help Busty however I could. The Castorana family held no fears for me. Busty's uncle was nothing more than a farmer despite rumours and reputation and his son Ross had always proven to be a gutless wonder when things got tough.

"There is no disrespect Mr Castorana. Busty will be here when he can. They still haven't found little Stella."

He stopped, ignoring the disrupted flow of pedestrian traffic. "When he can. When he can. Is he a man who cannot do as he wants to do, or does he think I had something to do with this thing, this little girl, my niece? Gone? Dead?"

In my mind was a picture of Joe sitting on his grey tractor, wide-legged shorts presenting a full view of penis and sack, ragged straw hat balanced on his head. Al's comment at the time now brought a smile to my face. "Old Joe's like a stick with a sombrero on one end and a fuckin' dick on the other", he'd said.

I didn't try to hide my smile, nor did I care how it affected him.

"I said before Joe. There is no disrespect. Now can we go down to your bloody pub, have a beer and talk?"

We sat in the private bar of the Bull and Goat Hotel, scattered around the walls were engravings of zodiac signs with Capricorn and Taurus four times larger than the rest.

Even as a young journalist, the place had fascinated me. Set in the middle of China Town it attracted a full and varied cliental. Seated around a table at the far end of the bar, four women were discussing the heated seats in their latest SUVs.

"Yuppie housewives. All they can do is spend their husband's fuckin' money and pretend they're better than the rest of us while they try to fuck the barmen." Joe walked over to the mirror near the women, took a gadget from his pocket and proceeded to trim his nostril hairs. They all turned disapproving glances at him.

He stopped the operation and turned with a surprised look. "I'm asorry ladies but I gotta this stuff up here." He indicated his nostrils. "This a thing work real good, look." He held the buzzing instrument out towards them.

"Jesus Dad! You're gonna fuck this place up sooner or later". Ross watched the women walk out.

"Ah piss off Rosario. If they can't tolerate their inferiors, they should stay home."

"Yeah! And what if they never come back and they won't if they think we're ignorant wogs."

Old Joe winked at me, and I couldn't control my laughter any longer.

"Come on Boy." Joe indicated the barman. "They all know how big Vince's dick is. They'll come back."

Ross glared venom at me, walked through into the public bar and slammed the door.

We talked and drank beer, and after an hour, Ross interrupted. He wanted a private discussion with his father. This time, as Ross was leaving the bar he punched me on the shoulder and said "Tully I hear you're back on the farm. Never were much of a farmer, were you? Never were much of anything."

I quickly slid off the bar stool.

Joe put a hand on me and growled at his son. "Not now boy. He's still my guest."

He looked at me, "You fly home tomorrow and tell Sebastian I'll help if I can but what can I do? And you tell him if he accuses me of being involved, I'll kill him. I'll come to my father's old farmhouse, and I'll kill him".

This statement was worrying. I wasn't concerned for Busty; I knew if a showdown was to eventuate then it would be far more likely that Busty would do the damage and not Joe or Ross. I also knew I would support Busty.

He smiled and lightly slapped my face, "You were always a good boy Tully. Always good to your mother, always helped your father, always respectful, I've seen the job you did fixing up your father's old Farmall tractor better than new and because of that Ross will give you a phone number and an address where you can get a 1955 Zephyr convertible." He nodded slowly, "It was my car many years ago, it's yours now Tully, I'd love to see you fix it up like it was when I bought it." He sighed; I could see the concern in his face. "I don't understand this business either boy. Who's gonna touch a little girl? Busty's girl. We both know how bad he can be, you just tell him my men know nothing about it and nor do I."

"What are you talking about Joe? You just said you'll murder your own nephew. I don't think so mate. I think you're a bit soft from city living."

"I gave you two warnings Tully. You understand them both." He turned and began climbing the steps to his private quarters on the top floor. Ross gave me a piece of paper with a phone number and address, "Dad's old car, I don't know why he wants you to restore it, I could have done it."

I sat in my hotel room overlooking the Capitol Theatre. I planned to spend the evening doing nothing. I couldn't get my head around old Joe's threats. His men could only mean the crop-sitters and by now Busty would have paid them a visit. If he believed they had anything to do with Stella's disappearance they would probably be ploughed into a cane paddock by now.

I thought of phoning him or Rocky, but I had no answers. For his uncle to make threats as he did, he must be concerned about Busty. I wasn't worried about the threats and I was happy enough that Joe had nothing to do with Stella disappearing. I sent a text to Lyn asking what Busty had been doing. He rang me a few minutes later with a story that wasn't surprising. They had gone to the giant's footprint. Busty jerked the tripwire to bring out the crop sitters. One carried a pump action shotgun. When he recognised them, he lowered it. Busty walked up close to them, told them Stella was missing and asked if they'd seen her. They hadn't but went a step too far when they told Busty if he couldn't look after his kid, he shouldn't be asking them to nursemaid her.

Common sense dictates if you're going to punch with bare knuckles, punch somewhere soft. Not this time. Busty hit the gun-carrying tough man straight in the face. Lyn told me his head snapped back, he dropped the gun and fell in an unmoving heap. The other sitter, though heavier than his fallen mate, lifted his hands and stepped back.

"It was a simple question," Busty said. "Have you got an answer?"

The man shook his head. "No Busty. She hasn't been near us."

"Pick up your mate. Pack your gear and go. If you're still here tomorrow

I'll see you never leave."

Lyn told me it happened so fast all he could do was look. He said Busty was out of control.

"I know I saw an enormous, Illegal crop of cannabis Lyn said "I also understand a third party was responsible for the cannabis although I have no proof of this. Because I witnessed Sebastian Castorana destroy the cannabis, my report will indicate I believe Giuseppe Castorana was responsible for planting and cultivating the crop."

I broke into Lyn's conversation.

"Mate, Your report? You sound like a cop. You know what the situation is".

"I am a cop. I will have to make a report on what I witnessed and no matter what I understand; I must state exactly what the evidence is. If I indicate that I had suspicion of anything else, then I become implicated".

"Okay! So, you will say you believe Busty did not know?"

There was a long silence.

Then Lyn told me that's what would happen but Busty would be required to give a statement to that effect.

I felt like saying bloody cops were all alike, but I knew Lyn would do what he could to help.

I asked about the chances of finding Stella. Lyn told me he'd organised a search which had not found any trace of the little girl. Now he would have to question little Bobby and record Busty's version of events.

After Lyn's call I began to feel concern. I was pleased that Busty got rid of the crop sitters and the crop but I knew it would upset his uncle even more and Ross would be looking for just such action to justify belligerence.

The phone rang again. It was Busty. He told me he'd burnt the marijuana. He was coming to Sydney to tell his uncle that his crop was gone and there would be no more. He said he needed my backup because he was sure we would need to break a couple of heads.

We walked into the Bull and Goat. Joe and Ross were alone in the private bar. Busty wasted no time.

"I've come to tell you that your crop is gone and I won't have any more on my land"

Joe was hunched on the bar stool. Elbows resting on his knees. He looked like a tired old man. I wasn't fooled. He remained hunched when he spoke. Ignoring me, he looked at Busty.

"Sebastian, you come here. You come to my house. You tell me you destroyed my property, my money. Family doesn't do that to family".

Busty wasn't far from anger. Since Stella disappeared, anger was close. He closed his eyes and when he opened them he appeared to be calm.

"You're no longer part of my family. You've put my family at risk for years. No more Joe.

Don't come on my land again. Not you, not this bastard. He pointed at Ross. None of the people you pay money to.

Joe straightened and nodded to Ross who left the bar.

The original Castorana gave the farm to Busty to be held by his father Serifano until Busty's maturity. The proviso was that Busty worked it himself. Only the harvest could be contracted to others. The farm, by modern standards was small, hardly enough land cleared for cultivation to support a family. The uncleared areas were rocky and sloped. All through his teenage years he cleared the rocks himself. Day after day, year after year he picked up rocks and moved them on a large farm trailer to act as a base on the slopes. He then dug topsoil and loaded it onto the trailer and filled the slopes to make them workable.

He developed rock-hard slabs of muscle that had never reduced to flab.

Ross returned with a huge man. Small head, dull eyes, large shoulders and muscular arms.

I moved to stand beside Busty.

"Stand back Tully", Joe said. "This not your concern." He turned to Busty, "This is Angelo. He understands respect. He will give you a lesson now."

I winked and stood my ground. If I could prevent Busty from being bashed, I would.

Our code was always the best form of defence was attack. Busty took a long step forward with his left foot and crashed his right knee into Angelo's crotch. The knee connected with all the force Busty could muster. The path that took the pain to Angelo's brain was quick. With a horrible groan, he collapsed on his back.

"No mate! Don't kill him". I shouted. Busty was standing over him with a grim expression.

"He's just a moron who gets paid to frighten people. If you want to kill someone kill the prick that pays him."

Joe straightened and Ross moved backward. I moved to stand in front of Joe. Then Busty laughed.

"Never show your face near my home again." He said to Joe. Your crop sitters have disappeared. Your irrigation pipes and your crop are gone. I burned them. If you or your people had anything to do with Stella's disappearance, you'll be dead before you can make a will."

We left without another word.

I thought we should relax. We both needed time to think about what happened in the Bull and Goat. The hotel that was, in reality, half owned by Busty and therefore his children.

"This pub mate has to be worth millions," I said.

"I don't care," he answered "My father, before he was killed the night Simmo murdered Tony, was growing the dope so there would be enough money to get rid of his brother. He wanted Joe out of the farm and his life."

"Come on! Let's have a beer."

We sat at a table outside some Irish pub. I walked inside, came out with two bottles of Angkor beer.

"What's this crap?"

"Sorry mate, they didn't have XXXX."

We sat quietly and finished our drinks.

"Another beer?"

He looked vacantly at me.

"You want another beer?"

"Another dozen, two dozen. What does it matter?"

"It matters; we need to get home. We won't find Stella sitting here."

"Stella's gone Tully. I know she's gone. That's the reason I'm down here. Someone is going to pay. Someone will die, if it's not Uncle Joe and now I don't think it is, then you need to help me find them."

I had to distract him; take his mind off people dying.

"How do you know your father wanted Joe off the farm?"

"Grandma and Mum made sure I knew everything."

I nodded, said nothing.

"After Dad died, Joe kept growing the dope. Now I've had enough. I don't want my daughters involved in dirty money or anything it bought."

I told him I understood, I would feel the same. He wasn't listening; he was looking down the street. I followed his gaze. Walking toward us was Ross with three men, well actually two men and what looked like a teenager.

"Shit!" Busty pushed his chair back, "Ross is coming with a couple of tough boys, Looks like more trouble. I think I'll need you to watch my back. How do you feel about that?"

"Just look after your front mate. You don't need to worry about your back."

It started to rain. I thought we were in a bit of trouble. Three big men and one not so big to take care of. It wasn't going to be easy. Unlike the Kung Fu movies where the mob attacks one at a time, giving the hero a chance to finish with each one.

Four against two was almost impossible to deal with. One man just needs to cause a slight distraction, put his opponent off balance and the others have an open target. If they walk straight up and attack, they'll easily have us I thought. They didn't, Ross had to gloat.

"You two farmers are going to eat more than dirt today," He sneered.

Busty didn't hesitate. He lunged swinging his elbow up and forward. 125kg with momentum concentrated into one elbow was sure to do some damage. It did, the first of Rosses' mates went down without a sound. Ross jumped back. The smaller character slipped behind Busty and I saw a knife in his hand. I couldn't reach his knife arm, so I grabbed his shoulder and pulled. He was quick; he cut my forearm before I could do anything and started to spin back.

Busty had the second tough by the throat and was pounding a fist up into his stomach.

The vicious little creep with the knife was aiming to stab into Busty's kidneys when I managed to grab his arm. This time I didn't give him a chance. I jerked his knife arm back and up, dodging his slash. He tried to cut my face. I held the hand with the knife up, grabbed above his elbow and smashed his arm down onto my knee. I felt his elbow break. He screamed but that wasn't enough. He had cut my arm badly. I picked up the knife and slashed across his eyes, I missed; now I was really angry, his throat was open and waiting to be cut when someone grabbed my arm. A woman's voice was shouting.

"No! No! Stop!"

The rage faded. I had the creep by his shirt front pinned against the pub wall. There were tables and chairs scattered around. A woman was holding my other arm with two hands and shouting at me. I dropped the little thug onto the footpath. Busty came over, he was looking at me strangely.

CHAPTER 5

"It's good Tully, we're okay, calm down, Ross ran away and the rest of them aren't moving. Why is blood running off your fingers?"

The girl let go of my arm and glared at me.

"What were you doing?" she said. "You were going to kill him"

I handed her the knife. She was right; I was going to kill him.

"Come on, let's have a beer before the police come," Busty said.

A waiter from the Irish pub had been standing in the doorway during the melee.

He and another of the staff started straitening their furniture. The girl was checking on the recipient of Busty's elbow, she rolled him onto his side. The other one was kneeling, vomiting and trying to catch his breath. She looked at the waiter and asked him to bring three beers and a first aid kit. I was told to sit down before loss of blood caused me to faint.

The first aid kit came, then three glasses of Irish beer.

"Put your arm on the table." She told me. She sat on a chair beside me and none to gently cut my sleeve to expose the wound.

"This is deep, it has to be stitched." She opened the extensive first aid kit, rummaged and came out with a wicked-looking needle and some thread.

"What are you doing?"

"I'm going to clean your wound, it may hurt."

She laid the needle carefully on a cotton wool pad, dived into the box again and came out with a bottle of disinfectant liquid. I couldn't take my eyes off the wound cleaning. There wasn't anything gentle about her scrubbing actions either. She washed her hands with the disinfectant and snapped on a pair of white gloves. She washed the needle and threaded it then looked into my eyes.

"Hang on! What are you doing," I was feeling nervous.

"I'm a doctor; please keep your arm still."

I was more nervous. "You look like an angel love. You aren't going to hurt me, are you?"

"Call me love again and I will." She pushed the needle into my arm.

When I opened my eyes, my arm was neatly stitched, and she was wrapping on a bandage.

"You right mate?" Busty asked, "You fainted."

"No chance. I closed my eyes so the doc here could get on with her work."

"My name is Carmel, or preferably Doctor Holt. Certainly not Doc."

Busty bumped my shoulder. "Now you've upset Doctor Holt when she's trying to fix your little cut."

The violence had changed Busty. I couldn't understand. He was more relaxed, and it worried me.

"It's good," Carmel was looking at me, "It will soon start hurting badly. Rest your arm, best if you don't use it at all for a couple of days."

Her very dark eyes were mesmerising. I put it down to shock.

"What about the four cunts, sorry I mean men who attacked us?"

"Only three, one ran off. There are two police officers and ten pub patrons guarding them. Most of the people in the hotel saw what happened and are on your side."

"Okay, Doctor Holt; thank you. We'll talk to him now."

I turned my head to see two men in suits, obviously detectives.

"Leave him!" Carmel instructed, and the police obeyed, "Let him get over the shock. I saw it all so take my statement and let him recover."

Busty sat beside me while the detectives were interviewing Carmel.

"Don't tell them about Uncle Joe and Ross. Just say we were looking for someone in this Irish pub, let them believe it was nothing but a pub brawl."

While the police were interviewing Busty, Carmel sat with me at the table. "I asked if she would amend her statement, I told her we didn't want to hang around Sydney, we had to get back home. "Can you explain my cut some other way?"

She looked at me widening her eyes in enquiry. "Well, I'm a doctor and a witness, if you really want me to change what I told them I suppose I could say I saw you hit your arm on the umbrella pole, It has a couple of clamps that look dangerous. The police will believe me, but you'll need to explain why you want me to lie."

I told her the whole story starting with Stella's disappearance. She was horrified. "Your poor friend, how can he cope knowing his little daughter is missing?"

"He was a mess, but this episode has changed him and I don't like what it's done, it's as if he enjoyed the violence. As if he was looking for it."

She stroked my bandaged arm; it felt good like she removed the pain with her touch.

"OK, I'll tell the police I didn't see any knife, I'll say it was the blood that led me to believe a knife must have been involved. Now keep your arm still."

I thanked her and told her I would make it up to her.

"You seemed to be far too… I wouldn't say cultured but better educated than I would expect a street brawler to be." She had a faint smile, and I felt she was trying to be friendly.

I could see she was puzzled. "So why are you in Sydney? Your mate Busty looks as if he could handle his own family."

"I'm here to keep Busty out of trouble."

"So that was your one job. You didn't do that very well, did you?"

My arm was hurting. "I'm a farmer come journalist, come farmer. I'm a poor old boy from North Queensland. I'm not a bloody miracle worker."

She smiled, "From what I saw he doesn't need much help. He stopped those men easily and you ended up being stabbed."

Her eyes still fascinated me. "I was unlucky."

"I'm joking. Where in North Queensland do you live?" she rested her hand on my good arm.

"The most beautiful place you've ever seen. Give me your email address. I'll send you pictures and descriptions. You'll be on the next plane up. I will even teach you all you need to know about catching fish and growing sugar cane."

"I can't say catching fish is high on my bucket list."

"Just wait till you've tried it." I grinned, "Me teaching you will fill your entire bucket list."

She explained that there were a lot of things on her bucket list and while someone taking her out to catch fish was not one of them, it would be nice.

"We have the best beaches, beautiful creeks and amazing waterfalls." I don't know why I was trying to persuade her. Then I looked into her eyes again and knew I wanted to see more of her.

"You're selling the place to me; I think I would like to spend time up there."

"Great! You'll never regret it. I might even arrange a broken leg or two, so you get to stay in practice."

"Probably yours." She laughed.

We exchanged telephone numbers and email addresses.

She now became serious. "My grandmother was Aboriginal; I've heard stories about racism in North Queensland. Tell me truthfully. How do you feel about First Nations people?"

"We have a lot of what you call 'First Nations people' There are some fools with obnoxious ideas who are prejudiced and seem to think everyone should agree with them, but the average person is accepting of all people, we treat them on their merits or de-merits, so, at times, we call them things that you probably wouldn't like. When you come up, I'll introduce you to one of my best mates, He's a First Nations person, and he'll tell you I'm very gentle with him, or, I'm thinking, he might not, he's a bit shifty at times." I grinned, "Maybe I won't introduce you."

She nodded, "I'll wait to be convinced."

I told her she would meet some of my very good friends. One is the Senior Sergeant in charge of the local police station, and they were all bound to tell her stories she shouldn't take as fact, especially the First Nations man. I knew Al would take every opportunity to ruin my reputation as I would his in the reverse circumstances.

She frowned and squeezed my arm. "Tell me truthfully Mr. Jack. Will there be more trouble like I witnessed today?"

I wasn't confident that Ross, being the slime bag he was, would give up.

"No worries, North Queensland is a peaceful place, and call me Tully," I put on a brave face, "Busty will handle any problems and Lyn, the senior sergeant, will give us the full support of the law."

The detectives came to interview me. Carmel stood; she needed to go to work but made me promise I would email her. That was something I would definitely do; how could I ever forget those beautiful eyes?

I made a police statement to the effect that Busty and I were having a quiet beer when the three men attacked us. Neither of us mentioned Ross's part. That was something we would deal with later.

"We'll be going home as soon as we can, they've organised a search for Stella and we both need to be there." Busty was showing real concern now for his missing daughter. "I'll book the flight for tomorrow morning."

"OK mate but don't book it too early. I have somewhere to go in Newtown; we can go to the airport that way."

"You gonna tell me what important place you need to visit,"

"Your uncle Joe has given me his old Zephyr convertible. He wants me to restore it. It's apparently in a warehouse on King Street. I just need to see it before I decide."

He nodded, said nothing.

That night I received a phone call from Lyn. He told me we needed to come home quickly.

The police search found no trace of Stella, so he brought in Al's uncle.

Al required he and his uncle be left alone to search for tracks. They eventually revealed they found the tracks of two little girls climbing up to the waterfall but only one set of tracks returning. Lyn had talked to Bobby and he needed to formally interview her. Roxanne was very upset and insisted Busty be present. I assumed Lyn had told her the result of the tracking. He was caught in a very bad place. As might be predicted knowing Rocky, she threatened to punch Lyn if he tried to question Bobby without her father being present.

In truth, Bobby, Rocky and Busty's firstborn was the closest thing I had to a daughter. I knew Al and his uncle would not be mistaken. They were taught by ancestors whose ability to track was vital to their survival. Still, I had to ask Lyn if he was sure. He said yes and hung up the phone.

I was horrified by the picture Lyn's comments painted and hoped there was a solution. At the same time, I couldn't think what that solution might be.

We had a lifetime friendship; the four of us have always been able to work through any problems that arose. I just didn't know how we could get Busty through what I believed was coming.

CHAPTER 6

The next day we picked up a taxi and headed to Newtown after I called the number Ross had given me and received the OK to look at the car.

"So, what's this Zephyr of Uncle Joe's worth?" Busty asked.

"Depends on its condition, a perfect original one could be up to a hundred and fifty thousand. There weren't many imported into Australia."

"No shit?"

"This one must be almost perfect. Ross reckons he could easily restore it and we both know Ross couldn't restore a shovel handle."

The taxi driver dropped us at the address in King Street. It was an old warehouse. The door was open, and we could see a light inside. We walked through the door and up to the car. It was lit by two spotlights.

"One hundred and fifty thousand for that?" Busty wasn't impressed and to be truthful it wasn't a very stylish vehicle, but it was one of the rarest, post-fifties cars in Australia and that meant It was quite driveable and could easily keep up with modern traffic. Stopping might be a different matter, but I had no plans to drive it in Sydney.

After we walked up to the Zephyr, all the warehouse lights came on. I heard movement. Two men were standing behind us with guns pointed our way.

"Well, how about this?" Ross was standing behind his men, "Not very smart of you to wander in here where there's nobody around to witness anything,"

Busty tensed which alarmed me with two guns pointed at us.

"You want something, or are you just demonstrating how smart you are?" I asked

He walked up and slapped Busty's face keeping away from the pointed gun. Busty reached for him. A shot was fired that hit nothing. I grabbed Busty's arm. I didn't plan on getting myself shot and I knew that if we didn't control ourselves that might just happen.

"This is bullshit Ross," I said grabbing Busty's arm. "If you want to frighten us then you have,"

"I'm warning my favourite cousin here that, very soon, he's gonna find us visiting him at home and if he doesn't treat us with respect, his life will become very difficult."

They backed to the warehouse door. We followed them.

"Don't come near me or my home," Busty said, "If I see you I'll bury you in a cane paddock."

Ross took out his own gun and shoved the barrel under Busty's nose. "I'm going to enjoy teaching you some lessons."

They left.

"So, Ross has become a real tough gangster," I said.

"He's a gutless snake, always will be, he'll hide behind a couple of morons with guns but if he comes near the farm, he'll find his guns won't save him."

I hoped Busty was right and I knew I would do anything to protect Roxanne and the girls, still, I was concerned and Lyn's words were in my head. When they were given the police report, Roxanne and Busty's lives would be shattered I even forgot to be afraid of flying.

When Busty asked what was wrong? I didn't answer.

We travelled back to Townsville in silence. Rocky was waiting at the airport with a police document in her hand. She took Busty aside and spoke earnestly and quietly to him. He was showing signs of extreme agitation. The drive home was difficult. I knew they would both be in denial but still badly affected by Lyn's investigation.

I picked up my Land cruiser, said a brief goodbye and drove to my own farm expecting to be alone and lonely. Al and Lyn were both waiting for me. We made a solemn trio on my veranda with a carton of beer but not much conversation. After a while, for something to say, I told them of the run-in with Ross and his supposed tough men. Carmel's bandage was peeled off and my wound examined.

Lyn naturally asked what the result of the police report was. I told him it hadn't been finalised when we left.

"So, they allowed you to leave without restriction?"

I shrugged then nodded. "There were mobs of witnesses, even a doctor."

"Nice stitching on your cut." Al was impressed.

"My doctor did a wonderful job."

"Your doctor? You have your own Sydney doctor?"

"Yep! Top Sydney doctor, you might even get to meet her."

They weren't impressed, they hadn't met Carmel."

"What can we do for Roxane and Busty?" Lyn asked.

"Do we need to confirm positively that Stella is gone?" I was searching for a way to soften the blow.

"There isn't any doubt mate. We read the signs; we actually saw more than Lyn told Rocky." He paused. "Tully, she didn't just fall that day, she was pushed, Bobby pushed her over the waterfall."

I was so shocked I couldn't speak for a time.

"I couldn't bring myself to tell Rocky." Lyn shook his head, "I couldn't even believe what Al and his uncle were telling me. I couldn't think straight then but it will have to go in my report and the detectives will want statements from everyone who was there that day."

I covered my eyes. "Hello darkness here we come."

Al got us a beer each. We drank them in silence. I wanted to talk to them about Ross and what we could do to cut short his vendetta. I knew, in the back of my mind, he would want revenge for the debacle at the Irish pub in Sydney. This wasn't the time. We had another beer each.

"Could you tell Rocky and Busty you are organising another search?" Al asked Lyn. "It would only delay the inevitable I know but some of us could search the top of the falls, and your policemen could check the cliff and George."

Lyn nodded, "Okay if Tully agrees to tell Roxane and Busty the whole story before the detectives do."

I had a very close relationship with both of them. I had once been in love with Rocky and I'd been Busty's best friend through school and since.

"I'll do it, but only when I think it's the right Time."

I wondered if it could ever be the right time. Everything had gone wrong with time. How long ago was it that we were all enjoying a day on the creek together? Less than a week. That day eventually brought disaster and each day since added something bad. I thought the next few days would bring the crisis and then a long recovery.

How wrong I was.

CHAPTER 7

The next day I called to see the grieving couple. I said we would keep searching for Stella in case she had crossed Waterfall Creek above the falls and couldn't find her way home. They showed no enthusiasm. They looked at me with blank faces.

Al and I decided to search the open forest on the opposite side of Waterfall Creek to Busty's farm. Lyn and the police searched the Gorge for Stella's remains.

I was a primary producer. Al owned a few acres and grew ten banana trees. Still, we were entitled to own and carry a firearm on our property. We both had 410-gauge shotguns, cut down to enable single-hand operation. I didn't like blundering onto a big brown snake without being able to defend myself. Al had a morbid fear of snakes. He'd been attacked as a young boy and the only reason he was still alive is his dog took the strike.

We started the search with a snake gun hanging from our belts in a special pouch.

Spreading to fifty metres or so we began. Neither of us doing much more than wandering.

There wouldn't be anything worth finding.

I heard a shot, and when I looked Al was waving at me.

"What's wrong?" I shouted.

He waved me over and pointed up into an old Scribbly Gum. Four metres up in the tree I saw an albino Koala.

"Shit mate, you trying to kill it?"

"No, you were walking off in the other direction. I had to get your attention. My mother always said there are white Koalas up here. My people's totem, my totem."

"Who the hell is shooting up here?"

We turned around. Labouring toward us through the grass we saw two beefy men in cheap suits, an unusual sight in North Queensland.

We looked at each other.

"Cops," Al said, "Checking on what we already told them or looking for taipans."

"Are you Tully Jack?" asked the shorter one with longer hair than I expected for a cop, He was looking at Al.

"No mate," Al indicated me with his thumb, "this pasty, white boy is Tully."

"You trying to be funny sunshine, you mob never know your place. What's your name boy?"

Al looked at me, there was going to be trouble. I shrugged, what could you do with a racist

"Albert Harvey," Al looked at the detective with a small smile.

"You're the fucken great Abo tracker the serge told us about, you solved the whole thing for us. Let's see your tribal scars. You bludgers are all a waste of time."

I took a couple of steps toward the loudmouth. I was half a head taller and ten kilograms heavier. I was hoping he'd prod me with his finger.

"I'm Tully Jack, you want something?"

The other detective diffused the situation. "Lyn… the serge, asked us to come up here and talk to you, you know the missing girl's family well."

I gave him a hard look, but he seemed to be more intelligent than the racist.

"And what were you shooting at?"

"Big brown snake, just to scare him, it's not legal to kill them, is it?"

He grinned, "I come from snake country and you're right, you can't kill them. Nothing wrong with a pellet or two up the arse to get them on their way though."

He looked at Al, "So Albert Harvey, you and Mr. Jack want to come with us down to our vehicle?"

The racist snorted, said nothing.

"I'm Detective Senior Constable Roland," he looked at Al, "also Harvey."

We shook his hand.

"This is Detective Constable Walker." We didn't shake his hand.

"We've got a billy and some tea back at our Toyota, "You want to come down, have a drink of tea and a chat?"

It was a request, not an order. We agreed.

We got the fire built and the water on with no help from the racist. I set the rocks for the fire, Detective Harvey collected wood and Al did the rest.

"Good to see the black boy's useful for something." The racist snarled.

Al took a step forward, "You're a loudmouth, pathetic prick that should have been drowned at birth." He was flexing his shoulders, a prelude to violence that I'd seen before. I knew he could fight like a threshing machine. I wasn't worried, he would have no difficulty with the racist and if Detective Harvey tried to intervene, I would stop him. The racist was about to be taught the error of his attitude, and I was looking forward to being a witness.

Detective Harvey strode over. I put my hand on his shoulder. "Leave it, old mate he's in line for a lesson and I'll make sure he gets it."

The racist lunged straight into two punches in the face from Al and another as he fell into the fire. He was fortunate the water hadn't time to heat and actually extinguished the flames before they did him any great harm. No one helped him up. He rolled onto his side and struggled to his knees. "You fucken black bastard," he mumbled through blood and swelling lips, "You'll be in jail for this."

I grabbed his hair and hauled him onto his feet. "You won't have a job for this sunshine."

"Alright, everyone, settle down," Detective Harvey had a grin on his face, "Detective Walker, go and sit in the car and clean your face. Mr. Harvey, you didn't have to do that to him."

"The pathetic prick is lucky he dropped before I really hit him. You expected me not to defend myself?"

I said, "Al here is a renowned filmmaker and a very good friend of your Senior Sargent. If I were him, I'd certainly be shafting your racist mate there."

He grinned again, "I think Al already shafted him. I've never seen quicker punches in my life."

"Our drink of tea is gone. Why did you want to chat to us?"

"You're not being officially questioned you understand?"

We waited. "I'd like to know what Sebastian Castorana's relationship with his daughters was like." He was looking at me. "And to be honest I'd like Al to go with me to the top of the waterfall and point out exactly how he and his uncle could read enough in the tracks to come to the conclusion that they did."

I saw the reason for the questions, "You understand that all I can give you is my opinion of Busty's home life."

"Apparently, you're his best friend. Your opinion will hold a lot of weight."

"He was attacked when he was a small boy; His brother was raped and murdered in front of him. He couldn't protect his brother then, now he would protect his wife and daughters with his life I can only imagine how much love and affection he has for them. I know I wouldn't like to threaten them in any way."

"Do you know if he held any one of his daughters above the others or showed more affection for one?"

This was something I need to consider carefully, "Stella, his second daughter was premature and very, very small. I think this worried both Roxanne and Busty, so they gave her a lot of attention. They bought her a doll with 'our special child' written on it but, since then she grew rapidly and they had two more daughters."

He nodded, "Anything else?" I shook my head.

"Will you and Al come with me to the top of the waterfall?"

Al grunted, "You want me to show you how to track like one of my Mob?"

"I just want to get everything straight. This is a terrible situation; I haven't some across anything like it ever. Come on we'll pick up Walker on the way. We used the tourist road to drive up this side of the waterfall because Lyn asked us not to go through Busty's property."

CHAPTER 8

We walked down to the police Land Cruiser through the grass, Detective Harvey leading. He stopped suddenly and waved us back. I saw the ugly head of an angry taipan. I grabbed at my snake gun as it lowered its head and started to move off. Not expected behaviour from a taipan. Normally it wouldn't hesitate to launch into a high strike. One of the main reasons they are so dangerous is their bite is high on the body. No chance of using a tourniquet.

We watched in disbelief as the Detective grabbed the snake's tail, pulled it out of the grass and flicked it like a whip. Breaking its back close to its head. Astonishing as it was, the act was incredibly dangerous. An hour away from any chance of antivenin, a bite was death.

Al walked over and looked at the snake, "The nasty bastard's dead alright, you've done that before I reckon."

The detective just shrugged. "My father was a snake handler, had his own show. There's not much I don't know about snakes. For instance, poisonous snakes don't climb trees. They can climb a tree no worries it's just they hunt on the ground because their prey lives mostly in borrows under the ground. I've often relocated bad snakes, and I do that by sending them to a better life if you know what I mean."

Al and I both knew exactly what he meant, even though it wasn't the accepted thing or even the legal thing, we nodded.

I put my snake gun back on my belt. He nodded towards the gun. "We'll have to have a talk about that gun before todays over, you too Mr. Harvey."

"What do you want to know? We both understand that we can't take our firearms outside our properties."

"They don't look to be a legal size and just who cut them down for you?"

"It was a man called Seaton...or Eaton?" Al looked enquiringly at me.

"No, Bacon, I think." I answered.

"OK. I understand you're not going to tell me, but you can't stop me from measuring them."

"You don't need to worry Mate," Al said, "They're legal. He told us they're a piss whisker over the right length. That's a scientific measurement if you're wondering."

We arrived at the police vehicle and drove to a tourist area where we were able to cross the creek above the falls. We made our way down to the waterfall, the two policemen leading.

When we were close to the lip of the George a call came through on the police radio. It was Lyn. He talked briefly and Harvey told us he had found Stella's body. He also mentioned the police station had a report by Roxanne. She believed she had seen Ross in a Range Rover checking out the farmhouse. That was what I was afraid of hearing. If Ross came anywhere near the house Busty would kill him.

Detective Harvey called me aside. He explained that Lyn would take the body directly to the morgue. He also said Lyn wanted me, begged me to break the news to Roxanne and Busty. I felt cold but nodded agreement.

When we came near to the scene of the disaster, Al told us to stop, he would show us where to walk so we didn't obliterate whatever was still readable. The racist said nothing, but Detective Harvey asked about tracking skill and why Al could see things we couldn't. I told him we could see exactly what Al could see, we just didn't know what to look for. Even a skilled tracker with a lifetime of experience such as Al's uncle always preferred to have another tracker with him so they could discuss the signs before deciding what they meant.

I told them there was no magic in the way an Aboriginal could find his way in and out of the rainforest when unfamiliar with the area and they would only be familiar if shown by older men, they would bend and break branches as they went in, so coming back out was simple. The racist grunted. To me his face looked painful and would stay that way for a few days which is what he deserved.

Al drew lines and circles around and adjacent to specific marks and pointed out the two little girl's footprints coming up the ridge, heavy on the toe prints and one small set of prints going back down heavy on the heel print with occasional small skid marks. Then he showed us the area of scuffed ground where a struggle had taken place.

The racist grunted again. I think his eye was too swollen to focus properly.

Detective Harvey seemed satisfied; He turned to go back to the police vehicle. I said I would walk down the green ridge to Busty's farm. Al was happy to go with the detectives and be driven back to his house.

I was concerned by Rocky's sighting of Ross but would deal with him later.

I cut through the footprint; all around me were burnt marijuana plants. When I could, I'd bring up my father's old Caterpillar D2, which wasn't as good as new but almost and with a small set of disc harrows, clean up the area. Not an easy job among the trees but I'd destroy all trace of Joe Castorana's last crop.

I followed the headland through the centre of Busty's home paddock. The bottom section of the paddock was harvested and

Busty had ploughed and harrowed it because it would remain fallow until planting season next year. They were sitting on the veranda.

Rocky hugged me and cried tears on my shoulder. I wanted to hug Busty but that was something we didn't do.

I didn't know what to say nor how to say it so it just came out, "Lyn found Stella's body down in the gorge, I'm sorry, I'm sorry, just an hour ago."

Busty staggered into the house, bumping into the door jamb and barely remaining upright.

Rocky screamed and began punching my chest and shoulders. I knew what she was feeling, I could do nothing to help.

CHAPTER 9

I took the D2, on a trailer behind my working tractor, as far as was safe up the green ridge and had just offloaded it and the harrow when my phone rang. It was Rocky. She told me Busty was on his way into town to identify Stella, he would call to see his mother. I made a sympathetic noise, but she spoke over me. Saying he was then going to the pub. I knew he would be OK; a lot of the people in the pub would be his friends or at least understand what he was going through. He didn't enjoy drinking without good company so I was sure he wouldn't stay long and wouldn't drink very much.

Then Rocky asked if she could come to my house to talk with me. I told her I would be home in twenty minutes. I climbed on to the Fiat tractor and was rolling down the ridge when my phone rang again. I was a teenager the last time I had two phone calls in ten minutes. I braked the tractor and looked at my phone. It was Carmel. I certainly hadn't forgotten her, in fact I thought about her constantly, I just didn't expect a response from my emails so quickly.

I fumbled my phone, eventually pushing the right button. Her voice was faint, but I listened very carefully, even turning off the tractor. She was leaving Sydney at eight o'clock tomorrow morning. She needed to be picked up from the airport because it was more than an hour's drive to my farm, and I should have explained that to her. I answered that I planned to be there to drive her to the farm.

I parked the Fiat in the shed just as Roxanne arrived, we went inside, and I made coffee. Before I had a chance to have my first sip she said. "Tully, tell me what happened in Sydney?"

"Nothing! Nothing happened in Sydney."

She slammed her coffee mug down, it fractured, coffee splashed and pooled on the table.

"The Surry Hills police rang looking for Busty. They told me they'd finalised their investigation into the brawl. Because he didn't make a complaint, they couldn't do any more Tell me what brawl?"

I shrugged, "Rocky it wasn't anything to worry about, just a couple of heroes Ross sent to frighten us. Busty took two out in ten seconds. One of them had a knife. A vicious little worm that I had to put down before he stabbed Busty in the back. That's how my arm got cut." I shrugged again, "It wasn't a problem, and there were witnesses, good witnesses. You'll meet one of them tomorrow. She's the only one who saw the knife and she didn't mention it, so the cops thought it was just a brawl outside a pub."

She went into the kitchen, came out with a cloth and cleaned up the spilled coffee. "Did Uncle Joe know about it?"

"No, I don't think so, he was angry when Busty told him that his marijuana was burned but he's an intelligent man. He must have known the situation wouldn't last for ever so I'm certain it was only Ross who was responsible for trying to have us bashed."

"Do you think that Ross will try to cause more trouble for us?"

He's a pathetic, gutless piece of shit and always has been Rocky, you know that. I don't know how he could do anything to you."

Her shoulders sagged and the fire disappeared from her eyes.

"Busty's changed Tully, because of Stella he's changed. It's an awful situation and I'm totally heartbroken but Busty has hardly a sign of life left. One minute he is just sitting, brushing the front of his shirt aimlessly, a man bound for suicide, the next he is pacing and talking to himself."

As she said this Busty came through the door, "What are you telling her? Isn't she upset enough? She doesn't need to hear any of your bullshit."

He grabbed the back of my head and started to force it down toward the table. I gathered my strength and resisted the pressure.

"I'm telling her everything, whatever she wants to know," my voice was coarse with the effort of resisting him. "Nothing I told her is bad, you know that, so let me go or regret it."

"Why is she here, why come to see you, aren't I enough for my own wife?"

Rocky grabbed his arm, "Stop it Busty, let him go, I'll tell you why I'm here."

He relaxed the pressure and stepping back, let go of my head. When I turned, I could see tears in his eyes.

"Let's sit down and relax," I said as I rubbed my neck, "Just listen to Rocky, she's worried."

"This morning, I saw a Range Rover in the trees at the back of our house," Rocky sounded very concerned, "I'm sure Ross was one of the men in it, I'm worried Busty, why would he come all the way up here? I wanted to know if Uncle Joe had declared war on us for destroying his crop."

People often talk about sparkling eyes or lifeless eyes. I could never see any difference in eyes myself but now I swear I saw a change in Busty's eyes, they seem to come alive.

"Nope, it wouldn't be old Joe looking for revenge. If he sent Ross up here it would be to scout for a new growing area. Not that Ross could find his arse with both hands even after you told him where it is, come on, grab the girls and let's go home. I'll check it out when it gets dark; see if I can find him creeping around."

CHAPTER 10

I had baked beans on toast soon after they left. I noticed a spot or two of mould on the bread, but it scrapped off pretty well. After I'd picked up Carmel from the airport, I would need to do some grocery shopping, or we wouldn't eat.

I was waiting at a table in the café when Carmel's plane landed. I had coffee ready when she walked down the stairs and out of the Security area. I felt my chest tighten at the first sight of her and my mouth go dry when she smiled at me.

I stood; she came over and kissed me lightly on the lips. I must have looked surprised; she laughed and took my hand, "Have I startled you? I just felt like doing that."

I smiled and asked if she always does what she feels like. She answered, never.

We sat and drank our coffee. I looked into her dark eyes and felt compelled to say something romantic to keep the moment alive. Instead, I asked if she wanted a salad sandwich.

She shook her head, "I'm still trying to digest the breakfast they served on the aeroplane."

"You ate it?"

"Of course, it's free"

I nodded; I was learning that she is a practical, thrifty girl. I told her I had a nice surprise for her. She smiled and opened her eyes wide.

"We're going grocery shopping."

She laughed, "I can't wait, I travelled all the way to North Queensland to go grocery shopping."

In the car park we walked over to my vehicle. She walked around it smiling then looked at me. "This is yours? What is it? It looks like it should have a machine gun mounted on it."

"It's a Toyota Land cruiser fj40 with a later diesel engine, power steering and disc brakes.

I was proud of it; I'd even fitted special heated, suspension seats.

She nodded, "You couldn't afford a proper top, so you put a canvas one on it?"

"Anyway, "I said, "It's reliable, has good seats and I left the Rolls Royce at home."

She giggled, "This is going to be an experience."

We called into Woodlands Village to do the shopping. We talked about what to buy and bought exactly what Carmel suggested. At the checkout she stood demurely and nodded at the groceries. I was paying whether I wanted to or not. I grinned, it seemed very natural, and I liked it.

I loaded the groceries into the Toyota. She opened the driver's door. "I want to drive home, I've never driven a bumpy old four-wheel drive and I've never driven on a country road,"

"God help me," I mumbled.

She frowned at me; I had never in my life seen such a cute frown.

"I drive around Sydney; I'm a good, careful driver."

"No one in Sydney is a good, careful driver. Their sole aim in life is to get in front of the car that's in front of them. Their favourite hobby is changing lanes."

"What if I promise not to change lanes?"

I nodded OK; Carmel had control of the Toyota. I sat in trepidation and tried to look relaxed.

We drove out of Townsville and onto the Bruce highway.

"This is just like the M4 with no traffic, it's easy, I'm driving your favourite toy, how do you feel?

"Like I'm being lowered into my grave."

"Relax, look there's no traffic."

I started to settle. Carmel was handling the unfamiliar vehicle well and the traffic was light.

Eventually we passed the final set of traffic lights and were soon onto the two-lane highway.

I was relaxed now and enjoying the unfamiliar feeling of being driven. Twenty minutes later my phone rang. It was detective senior constable Harvey; he was at my house with Al and Lyn and wanted to see me, soon if possible. I told them I would be more than an hour.

Carmel looked at me with that spectacular frown. "We're only forty minutes away surely? Why did you say more than an hour?"

I laughed, "I love having a beautiful chauffeur, so long as she keeps her eyes on the road."

She ignored my flattery, telling me not to be flippant and demanding the truth.

I told her that from the airport to home was too far to bring ice-cream, so we have to drive into our local town where the deli keeps Ben & Jerry's Peanut Butter ice cream for me. We parked in front of the deli; Carmel looked at me opening her eyes very wide. I wasn't sure if this was her way of asking a question or if it was just a lovely expression.

"There are sides to you that I never imagined."

I tried to look as innocent as possible. "Come in with me, it's a small, friendly town, don't be surprised if they call me Uncle Tully, I have relatives in the deli."

I introduced Carmel as Doctor Holt. I knew in coming weeks I would have many questions to answer.

With a lot of goodbye Doctor and see you later Uncle Tul, we left.

"What a friendly, quiet town and so very pretty." Carmel was impressed.

"Lots of retired people with imaginary health problems who would love to see a women doctor. Probably a great place to start a practice."

"Perhaps you're right." Carmel got into the driver's seat smiling. I wondered if I would ever get my Toyota back.

"Do you know what I can't wait to see?" She said as we left town.

"Our beaches?" She shook her head. "A hard-working farmer busy working his farm?"

"No! The Rolls Royce you have in your shed. It will have so much more class than this machine gun carrier," she giggled, "Is it yellow?"

We arrived at the farm. I told Carmel I made up a room for her, clean sheets, air conditioning, TV, even a device to play music though I didn't know exactly what it was called.

"Oh, do I get to choose the music or is it your play list?"

"Mine I suppose."

"What music do you like?"

"Everything except what I don't like, I don't know, rock and roll, love songs, ballads, country,"

"Wow! I'm impressed, I suppose you sing too."

"I do, unkind people often ask me not to, but I think I sound OK."

She kissed me lightly, "I'm going to enjoy staying with you in my air-conditioned room listening to your special music."

I was feeling good, I knew I was in love, and then Al came out of the house and deflated my mood.

"Who's this?"

"This is my special Sydney doctor, the woman who saved my life when I was gravely wounded. Carmel, meet Al, Al this is Doctor Carmel Holt."

I could see Al was impressed, before he could say something I would regret I told him to grab a port and take it inside. That didn't stop him, he lifted a bag out and said, "Bout time you found a good-looking Sheila, last couple looked like cows, in fact they were cows, new blood for the herd." He walked onto the veranda laughing.

I looked at Carmel, she was also laughing. I struggled up the veranda steps with the other bag.

"Here, let me help," Lyn waited until I reached the top step before offering to help. Carmel carried her doctor's bag.

AL came out, "I put the doctor's port in your room. Isn't that where you took the cows?" He wasn't smiling but I knew laughter wasn't far away.

"OK, OK, the fun's over," I said before they could ruin my reputation completely, "what did you want to talk to me about?"

CHAPTER 11

"It's nasty mate." Detective Harvey put his hand on Carmel's back and guided her to a chair.

"These two blokes are cops, this is Lyn, he might look young but don't be fooled, he's not, it's just that his job is not very demanding. He calls himself a confirmed bachelor, we think that's because no woman would have him. The other one is Detective Roland Harvey, he doesn't look young. Gentlemen this is Doctor Carmel Holt."

She smiled at them.

"I'll get the groceries; see what Carmel wants to drink." I carried the groceries and ice cream inside, two trips, no offer of help.

Carmel was the centre of attention when I finally sat down. She had a cup of coffee, someone left me a beer, I would have preferred coffee.

"Tell me the nasty problem," I demanded.

"Before you do, what is a port?" Carmel asked.

I leant over and kissed her; I needed to show some degree of possession before they monopolised her completely. "She's a Sydney girl," I said, "She doesn't understand Queensland English." They nodded.

"The proper name for what you call a bag or suitcase is a port," Al explained,

I could see she didn't quite understand but she nodded. What a wonderful girl.

"Are you going to tell me what nasty business I'm involved in?"

"Your father's old Caterpillar's been burned," Lyn said

"Shit! How? That ridge wouldn't burn, water runs out of it all year."

"Someone deliberately set fire to the Cat," Al said, "they drained the diesel from the tank, pored some over the tractor and lit it."

"How much damage?"

"Not real bad," Al explained, "You'll have to reupholster the seat, that's the only upholstery on the thing, maybe replace some engine hoses and new paint, and probably the gauges will be buggered. They didn't use a lot of diesel so the fire wasn't intense."

"OK, I'll look tomorrow." I went into the kitchen and checked my wine cupboard; I had five bottles of Mateus Rose, my favourite, and seven bottles of Pepperjack Shiraz. I opened the rose.

Carmel came in, "I'll have a shower and go to bed Tully, I'm really tired." She kissed me on the lips, "Today has been nice, thank you."

I watched her walk down the hall, the burnt Caterpillar forgotten.

We sat on the veranda and drank the wine, between four of us it didn't amount to much.

Thirty minutes later Carmel came out, "Tully I tried your music, Frank Ifield's 'I remember you' really? Not what I'd call bedroom music." They laughed. I happened to like Frank Ifield, 'The Wayward Wind' I'd call a classic.

Carmel was still smiling, "From there we went to Air Supply's 'Love and Other Bruises'

Another great Aussie talent, well one of them at least, but to my mind, not bedroom music either. Maybe tomorrow we can enjoy Chuck Berry." She laughed and disappeared.

I asked Lyn if he told Busty about the burnt tractor, he had and Busty went up the green ridge with Al to check, Al told us there were heaps of tracks, especially on the wetter patches of ground, three men were involved, and they had drained the tank but hadn't used very much diesel to start the fire. Apparently Busty said he knew exactly who was responsible and where they came from.

Lyn thought Busty would go looking for the men and that concerned him.

Remembering Carmel's forceful statement that her grandmother was Aboriginal, I asked about the racist detective.

Lyn looked grim, "I've had complaints about him before. Hearing what Rolly here and Al had to say I decided to give him an ultimatum."

I nodded, "Yes, how did that go?"

"To be honest I was tempted to punch the worm. In the end, knowing his career was finished, he resigned, He did make threats about all Aboriginal people and he especially threatened you and Al."

That pleased me. The last thing I wanted was a cop with Walker's attitude involving himself in my life. His threats didn't worry me, and Al had already proved that handling former detective Walker wasn't difficult.

I decided I would take Carmel to visit Rocky and Busty in the morning and then we would go up to assess my burnt D2. My visitors finally left. The house was quiet, no music coming from Carmel's room; I listened at her door and resisted the urge to open it. Before I could walk away Carmel came out. She touched my face, "My door won't be locked Tully, but I would like a little more time with you before we commit to anything."

I awoke next morning to the smell of coffee. Carmel was using the Nespresso machine.

I walked into the kitchen with no shirt on. She ignored my display and that was deflating so I took out the frypan and asked if she liked sausages and beans for breakfast. She gave me a quizzical look and claimed she'd never heard of sausages and beans for breakfast.

I told her she was about to have a wonderful new experience.

After breakfast I dressed, and we had another coffee on the front veranda. Late September was bringing very warm weather.

"it's beautiful," Carmel said, "really beautiful, I can't believe I can hear birds, and what's that sweet perfume on the breeze?"

"Sugar, it's newly cut sugarcane you can smell and tomorrow the contractor will be harvesting that paddock beside the house, it will be noisy, but you'll find it interesting at least for a while."

We finished our coffee, and I asked her to wait for a few minutes and I'd bring out my Rolls Royce. I walked around to the shed; one section was closed. I opened the doors and inside was my father's fully restored, gold, 1967 Ford Falcon GT. Beside it a magnificently restored Farmall tractor. I thought about presenting her with the Farmall then I wondered if she would understand the joke. I drove the GT around to the front of the house. Carmel walked down and around the car; she opened the door and slid in, a very solemn look on her face.

"This is definitely not a Rolls Royce."

I gave a palms up shrug.

She smiled widely, "It's better, much better," She reached over the gear shift and hugged me.

I couldn't miss the opportunity and held her face to kiss her,

"You're full of surprises Tully and I love...."

I kissed her too soon. I was sure she said I love you. I hoped I wasn't wrong but what if she didn't? I looked into her beautiful, ebony eyes and desperately hoped she said it.

"Where are we going to go in this beautiful car?"

CHAPTER 12

"I thought we'd go to Busty's place, you could meet Roxanne, it's a terrible, heartbreaking time for her and maybe you can help."

Carmel nodded, "I'll try, poor girl, I can't imagine how badly she must be suffering."

"I'm afraid Busty might go looking for the bastards responsible for burning my D2 and I want him to know that I'm not worried about the burning, it will give me another project to keep me busy during the growing season."

We drove into Busty's yard. "She has a beautiful house."

"What? Nicer than mine?"

"Well, a bit."

"It started out almost exactly the same as mine. The same carpenter built them both. Serifano, Busty's father practically rebuilt it with money from their marijuana crops. Busty's father and uncle and grandfather have been growing the stuff since the 60s. Busty ended it the day Stella disappeared."

"Was he part of it?"

"No! Just Giuseppe his uncle and his cousin Rosario. Old Joe is a crook for sure, but Ross is a worm."

"Ross is the one who ran away from your fight in Sydney isn't he?"

"Yea, that's him, as I said he's a worm, but he's got a pocket full of money and Rocky thinks she saw him hanging around the house."

Roxanne greeted us at the door and when I introduced Carmel, she was extremely friendly, which was unusual when she met my friends. After a glass of wine, Rocky's mood was changing; I noticed tears in her eyes. Carmel also noticed Rocky's visible emotion.

"Can we help? Tell us what we can do."

Rocky wiped away her tears, "We had two detectives here this morning, the local man Harvey and a chief inspector from Brisbane, a public prosecutor, whatever that is. He told us Stella was probably murdered, and Bobby is their only suspect."

I looked at Carmel, I didn't know what to say or do.

Carmel hugged Rocky, "I'm sure they must be wrong."

"It was Al. He showed them the tracks, the only evidence they have is the tracks. It's all Al's fault, if he kept quiet it would be OK." She began to cry.

I started to say something; Carmel shook her head and continued to hug Rocky. I knew she didn't mean to blame Al, and I knew he would be horrified to hear her; he was just doing what the police asked of him.

Finally, she stopped crying. "Busty's gone with the police up to your burnt tractor, Detective Harvey wants to examine the scene and start an investigation."

Carmel stood up and held my hand, "Tully will they need you up there?"

I nodded, "I suppose I should go up, being cops they'll have a million questions," I was going to mention Al's summary of the fire but decided I shouldn't mention him. "Bugger it, let's have another glass of wine," I took the glasses and bottle out onto the veranda. "Come on, we might as well enjoy the weather and the silence while we can, the harvesting contractor will be cutting the rest of your house paddock as soon as he's finished at my farm."

Carmel came close to me and whispered, "I'll stay with Rocky."

I nodded and she kissed my ear.

We sat for a while with no conversation, and then Carmel asked to use the bathroom. When she had gone Rocky put her hand on my shoulder, "Tully, that girl is in love with you, God help her. Look after her she's a wonderful woman, don't you hurt her."

I shook my head, "I'm in love with her Rocky, there's no chance I'll hurt her."

"Was she working before she came up here?"

Carmel came out, her thick, black, wavy hair brushed and if possible, shining more than ever.

"Rocky's being nosey, she wants to know your life story."

I was pleased and relieved to see them both smile,

"Tully, Carmel gave me her wide-eyed look, why don't you go and help the police look at your father's burnt tractor? Rocky and I will stay here and chat, perhaps have another glass of wine, even two if we feel like it."

I was being dismissed, "OK, I'll be back soon."

CHAPTER 13

I drove up the green ridge as far as I was prepared to take the GT and then walked for ten minutes. Busty was sitting on the burnt grass beside the Caterpillar, I sat down with him.

After a few minutes he asked, "How's your new girlfriend?"

"She's great mate, she's the doctor who stitched my cut arm. How did you know she was here?"

"Detective Harvey said she is staying with you; said she is a doll. From memory he's right.

Only you could end up with a girlfriend because of a tiny cut like you had."

"What did the cops say about my D2 being burned?"

"They say it was deliberately set alight; someone drained all the diesel from the tank and used it to burn the tractor."

That was puzzling, I knew my father fitted a modified fuel tank that held eighteen gallons, and I remembered filling the tank. I told Busty that the tank was full so they used only a small amount of diesel to burn my tractor, or the blaze would have been very fierce and done far more damage than it did.

"What the fuck does that matter?" Busty's mind was somewhere else, I didn't blame him.

"Are you pissed that they stole your fuel as well as burning your tractor?"

"I am, but my real problem is what happened to the rest of it? Seventeen gallons is no light load to carry away. They must have had a reason."

"Who gives a fuck Tully? Who cares what they did with it?"

I stood, "you're right, come on lets go home."

"You know what that cop from Brisbane told me? He said they believe Bobby killed Stella. How am I going to live with that? How can Rocky live with that? The police won't do anything unless we want counselling. Bobby is too young to even think about prosecuting, I don't know how we can look at her every day and not know what she might do, what will our lives be like?"

I had nothing to say. Where could I find answers for him?

I saw strange shapes and shadows in the trees screening the footprint. I walked into the belt of trees, I was sure I saw movement, so I went further in, something hard jammed into my back. Ross was standing in front of me with another man I didn't recognise.

"You're fucked Jack," Ross grinned, "You've got a gun in your back and a man who knows how to use it." He punched me on the mouth, I saw it coming and pulled my head back, that took some of the force out of the blow, but I felt my lips split against my teeth, I was angry.

A voice beside my ear told me I was going to get my lights punched out, then I heard a painful grunt, and the gun pressure disappeared. I dropped to elbows and knees; a figure leaned over me then suddenly jerked back. I launched myself up, my head hit Ross under the jaw, it hurt and made my ears ring. Ross collapsed; his brain had stopped sending messages to his joints. I swung towards the other man as he turned away, I was too slow, Busty grabbed him by the side of the neck and slammed a fist into his face, everything he had went into that blow. When I looked around there were three men on the ground and Busty was holding his fist.

"You bugger your hand mate?"

"It feels a bit sore."

"Who was the one with the gun?

"That's our local detective."

"OK, not a detective any longer, Lyn told me he quit with a bit of persuasion. How many times did you hit him?"

"Just once in the kidneys, he'll be pissing blood for a week, I took the gun off him first just in case he shot you."

"Thanks, I appreciate your thoughtfulness, come on, let's go to your place, Carmel's there with Rocky, she'll fix your hand."

He smiled. The adrenalin must have taken his mind off the horror of Stella's death.

"That's a pretty handy girl you've got there, you need to hold onto her."

I looked at him, "You just remember to call her Doctor Holt, not love or Doc, she'll be in a good position to hurt you if you upset her."

"Don't worry, I'll show her plenty of respect."

We walked down to my car, I said "hang on mate, where's the gun? If we're leaving those morons back there, we don't want to leave the gun with them."

He took it out of his pocket, "here, you take it."

It was a Colt police positive 38 revolver. I opened it, removed one bullet and rested the hammer down on the empty chamber, then dropped it on the floor in the back seat of the car

CHAPTER 14

We walked up the stairs at Busty's house. The women were sitting on the veranda.

"You two lovely ladies still drinking wine?" At least that's what I instructed my mouth to say. They looked at me blankly and then Carmel Jumped up, she touched my face, "What have you done?"

"Bumped into a branch," I explained. I don't think my words were clear and if they were they weren't believed. Carmel looked at Rocky who was shaking her head.

"Look at him," she indicated Busty who was holding his swollen, misshaped hand. "I don't think he caught that hand in the car door."

Carmel looked at Busty's hand, "Do you have a first aid kit? I didn't bring my bag."

Roxanne quickly disappeared inside and returned with a comprehensive, survival kit.

Carmel gently touched my damaged lips, "I'll see what I can do for you." She rummaged through the first aid box and found a dressing, after cutting it in two she poured a solution on it and smoothed it onto my lips. "Hold it there carefully while I look at Busty's hand."

She told him to sit beside his wife and began examining his hand. "Your finger is dislocated, I'm afraid I will have to hurt you so be prepared." She squeezed and moved his finger, "I don't think It is broken but you really should have it X-rayed and an MRI scan."

"There's nothing wrong with it," Busty growled, "It's just a bit bent. Please Carmel, Doctor Holt, straighten it and it'll be good."

She continued to examine his hand, "OK, kiss your wife while I manipulate it."

Rocky grabbed his face and kissed him. Carmel wriggled and then jerked the finger. Busty gasped and it was all over.

"Ice it for an hour or two, then I'll tape it to the next finger and that's all I will be able to do."

I was about to tell her how great she is. She told me not to talk as she removed the dressing from my mouth.

"Doctors are very bossy." Busty said. We all glared at him then Carmel laughed,

"I think I might need to manipulate that finger again."

Busty grinned, "I'm just saying. Nothing personal Doctor Holt."

She gently ran her fingers over my lips, "Good there isn't any real damage, I think a kiss will fix your lips better than anything." Which she proceeded to do.

I pulled her closer; she giggled

"Tully, careful, you'll hurt your mouth." She said, "But not too careful"

Right then I didn't care about my mouth, I wanted her, it was such a powerful feeling. I whispered, "Soon Carmel, I love you." She hugged me and whispered, "I love you too Tully."

I wanted that embrace, that moment to last forever.

"If you two have finished whispering, would you like a drink?" Rocky was smiling broadly.

Carmel broke our embrace, "If you and Busty would like to come over tonight, I'll cook my special fried rice and baked potatoes and I'll check Busty's finger and tape it."

Rocky seemed surprised, "Of course we'll come, won't we Busty?" Busty grunted.

"And Tully," Carmel said, "I want to drive your fabulous GT home." I handed her the keys.

Roxanne and Busty arrived a few hours later, "I'm surprised you're not in a suit and fucken tie," Busty said.

I laughed, "Just because this is the first time the richest farmer in the district and his lovely wife have ever come to dinner at this poor old boy's house."

"It's the first time we've been invited," Rocky said. "Will we be eating at your mother's Grand old dining table?"

"Of course, look, it's the first time the table's had a cloth on it since Mom left. Carmel had to search but she found one." I took a bottle of Mateus from the refrigerator and filled the glasses.

"What does Carmel think of cold rose?" Busty asked. Carmel came out of the kitchen, "I love it, I'm an Aussie and I'm in North Queensland. The only people who don't like cold reds are strange little people from small, cold countries in Europe or fools who want us to believe they are wine connoisseurs."

We ate, as different as fried rice and baked potatoes sounded, it was perfect. Desert was something called Angels Breath. I watched as Carmel made it, flavoured jelly crystals,

A bit of water and evaporated milk. Her Aboriginal grandmother's recipe she said. It was also very good.

"Does anyone want to listen to Frank Ifield?" Carmel asked with a smile. I was outvoted; we didn't listen to Frank Ifield. We settled down with a glass of rose and coffee.

"Now," Rocky said, "please tell us what happened today?"

Busty grunted, he wasn't saying anything.

"Who's looking after the kids?" I asked.

"My parents, I took them there last night when I knew that detective from Brisbane was coming, I'll pick them up tomorrow." I could see tears starting in Rocky's eyes.

I told them the whole story of my ambush by Ross and his mates and how Busty rescued me.

"Why has all this happened Busty? Is Uncle Joe so enraged at the loss of his future marijuana crops that he's looking to bash or even kill you? What did you do in Sydney? What did you say to the criminal bastard?"

"It's not Uncle Joe, Rocky, I told you before. It's Ross and I'm certain he's just being a vindictive mongrel. He hasn't enough guts to do anything on his own, so he's hired a couple of tough guys to hide behind. Tully didn't tell you but when we left them this morning, they were all on the ground and Ross had a broken jaw from the top of Tully's thick scull giving his jaw a bump,"

"He's right," I said, "all of them will be in hospital tonight. Before you came over, I rang Al and asked him to check with his girlfriend, the nurse from the hospital. He hasn't let me know yet, but I don't think we'll have any more trouble from them."

"So, nothing serious happened in Sydney?" Rocky was worried, she must have been struggling to cope with losing Stella and all that situation brought into her life. I wanted to ease her mind as much as I could.

"Rocky, Carmel can tell you, she witnessed the incident, it didn't last more than a minute or two and even then, Ross disappeared in case we went looking for him. It's just Ross trying to be a standover man when he isn't even a man."

They were obviously ready to leave. Carmel hugged each of them, "Before you go to bed tonight, hug each other, a long hug with kisses. You'll feel better."

Rocky smiled a week smile, "We will Carmel."

Busty's smile was a little better, "Thank you, I hope this oaf is treating you good because I think you deserve better than him." His smile grew wider, "we will definitely hug tonight but it won't be before we go to bed, no bed for me, I'll be going up the ridge to wait in case Ross turns up, then I'll be having a word with him."

Rocky's smile disappeared, "Busty, why not stay with us, we are the ones you should be looking after."

CHAPTER 15

Next morning I received a phone call from Al. He was up on the high ridge across from the falls where we found the albino Koalas, and he could see smoke coming from Busty's farmhouse. He thought he could see figures down there. I told him to ring the fire brigade, and I would go straight to the house.

Carmel and I took the GT and quickly drove over to Busty's farm.

I could see smoke coming from the house, a Range Rover was parked across the driveway, and I couldn't get around it without knocking down one of Busty's gate posts. I'd helped erect those posts and knew knocking one over would not be easy.

Carmel could also see the smoke and she urged me to stop so we could run to the house.

I ended with my grill almost touching the Range Rover's back door. The smoke was getting thicker and then I saw a figure walking towards us with a shotgun held out.

"Quick Carmel, roll over the seats and lie on the back floor, I'll get out to distract him." She'd seen the man with the gun and scrambled over the seats as I climbed out.

I stood beside the car. The man approached; it was Walker the ex-cop. He came closer and I was starting to ask him if they were putting out the fire when he hit me with the gun butt just behind my ear. I didn't expect it and dropped stunned to the ground.

"How does that feel, you pathetic bastard," He screamed and shot the windscreen out.

"Get up bastard; watch me wreck your golden fucken car." He pumped another shell into the breech and shot the driver's window.

In my befuddled state I thought I could hear screams coming from the house. I tried to stand; He clubbed me again. "You wanna help your mate's wife and kids? Well you can't, they're burning right now." He shot the window of the rear door. "I blew their knees off, all of them, they screamed, you should of heard the screams. They're dead and you're gonna be dead. He shoved his face through the shot out rear window

"First you're gonna watch me fuck up your car."

I heard another shot but not from his shotgun. His head snapped back in a mist of blood and other stuff. He crumpled to the ground beside me. There wasn't much left of his lower face. I didn't know what happened, I had a tremendous headache, and I vomited. I could still hear screams coming from the house, then the car door burst open and Carmel scrambled out, the gun I'd thrown onto the floor of the car the day before, was in her hand.

"Quick!" She shouted, "There are people in the house."

I grabbed at the car trying to get my legs under me. Eventually I was able to stand but I was unstable and needed to support myself.

"Hurry Tully, quickly." She started running to the house, the colt still in her hand. I picked up the shotgun and staggered after her with a terrific ringing in my ears. I saw Ross come from the back of the house. Carmel also saw him; she shot at him without hesitation. I had a far better chance of hitting him with the shotgun, but I couldn't manage to pump another shell into the breech. He disappeared back around the far side of the house, skirting wide to avoid the flames. I yelled to Carmel, "Around there," Indicating the near side of the house beside the cane paddock. As I tried to run to her my legs stopped working and I fell. I was sliding and dragging myself toward her as she went down the side of the house. She came back. "There were two of them and they went into the cane." She helped me to my feet; everything was sort of dark and blurry around the edges and my head ached so much I couldn't think.

"Tully, the house is blazing everywhere. I heard people screaming before. If that animal did shoot them in the legs." She started crying. I held on to her, I had tears in my own eyes as I watched the house burn. I tried to distract her, "Carmel, you shot a man, are you OK?"

"That wasn't a man that was a piece of dirt, a germ, an animal that looked like a man and he was going to murder you. I'm grateful I had the chance to stop him. I was lucky you had a gun on the floor of your car."

That revolver surely saved our lives. Walker would have found her without doubt as he was shooting my car to pieces.

With head down she asked, "Do you think they were all inside?"

I said nothing.

Carmel put her hands up to her face, she still held the Colt. "Who could do that? What sort of mind would even think to do that, shoot people so they couldn't move and burn them to death?" She sank down. I was using her for support, so I also went down. We stared, horrified at the burning house.

Distant sirens brought us back to the reality of the situation. The driveway remained blocked by the Range Rover and my car. The fire truck pushed through Busty's post and rail fence then stopped at the corner of the house closest to the cane paddock and two metres away from Carmel and me. The house was still burning, beyond saving. The firemen and women unravelled their hose and started a pump. I was surprised to see them drive down between the house and the cane and extinguish the patches of cane that had caught alight. I suppose in a sugarcane district they knew how bad a cane fire could be.

A police car came through the gap in the fence made by the fire truck and stopped well back form the house out of the firefighter's way.

Lyn and a constable got out. I tried to stand up.

"No, stay there mate, the house is almost gone, Busty will be devastated."

"He might be in there." I said

Lyn was watching the fire, "In the house, it's almost completely burnt, why would anyone be in there?"

CHAPTER 16

"We think people were in the house, we could hear screaming, and Walker told us Roxanne and the kids were in there."

He looked at Carmel; she nodded without looking at him.

I put my hand to the side of my head where the first blow from Walker hit. I could feel blood in my hair and on my hand, my head still ached,

"Come with us." Lyn said, "there's more to this than an unexpected fire." I stood and stumbled. He stopped me from falling.

"Whoa! Hold on boy. What's up?"

Carmel jumped up and put her arm around me, "He's been bashed on the head, twice. Look at the blood, he can't stand up, help him over to the cars."

We went a few paces then I had to vomit again. My vision seemed to be clearing. We struggled around the front of the Range Rover. Lyn let go of me, "What the fuck happened to your car? Who shot Walker?"

I looked at Carmel, she pushed her hair back, "please open the car boot, I want my medical bag, Tully needs attention and rest."

Lyn was always patient; it didn't matter if he was trolling a lure behind his game boat waiting hours for a big fish strike or doing police work. He dutifully opened the boot and brought Carmel's bag to her and then he shouted to the constable who was walking around the burning house and beckoned him over.

"I need a statement from each of you, right now while your memory is fresh."

Carmel ignored him and carefully cleaned my wounds then rubbed ointment on them.

"What's that?" I asked.

"Its paw paw and aloe vera ointment,

"Really paw paw?"

"Yes, paw paw, it should stop the bleeding and limit the possibility of infection until I can shave you and put a proper dressing on." Then she cleaned my face and kissed me.

"Hey! Stop that." Lyn commanded, "Witnesses shouldn't collude, and kissing is definitely not allowed."

The constable laughed and looked away catching sight of Walker's body at the back of my car.

"Shit Sarge, what's this? It looks like Walker's been shot."

Lyn waved a hand at him, "Take out your notebook, we'll interview our witnesses."

"I'll talk to you now Senior Sargent Smith. If I must. Tully can be interviewed when I, his doctor, say he can."

Lyn nodded, already he understood when Carmel spoke as a doctor she expected to be obeyed. "Ok, please start at the beginning. Tell me how you knew the house was on fire?"

Carmel gave a full account starting with the phone call from Al telling us he could see smoke around Busty's house and going through to the shooting of Walker. She told how he came to my car, clubbed me, and shot the glass out. She repeated his boasting, how he shot Roxanne and the girls in the legs so they couldn't escape the fire. The constable wrote it all down and Lyn made no comment. His phone rang, after wandering about talking for some time he came back. "Al is still up on the high ridge the other side of the falls; he's been photographing the white koalas and the country around them for his mother and he says Busty was up near the footprint earlier in the morning. Al saw him with a shotgun. He also says he heard a shot.

I couldn't make sense of that. Last night Busty told us he was going to find Ross, but the Range Rover is down here at the farmhouse right beside us, Ross wouldn't be up at the falls.

Lyn was a cop; He had training and years of experience solving problems and working out scenarios to fit the circumstances. "I think they knew Busty would be up there when they planned the murders. One or two of them came down from the tourist road across the creek above the falls. They were going to spin Busty a story to get him down here."

"What about the gunshot Al heard?" I asked.

He shook his head, "Their story didn't work and an altercation developed. Busty must have shot at them." He indicated the pump action gun I'd left on the lawn, "That's Busty's full choke duck gun from when it was OK to shoot ducks. They must have taken it off him."

"What are you thinking Tully?" Carmel asked her dark eyes wide.

"I'm just hoping he's not lying up there somewhere wounded and needing help."

"I saw them go into the cane Tully; they probably went up there. Don't go there please, don't risk your life, I've just found you Tully, please stay here."

Lyn said, "I think we need to find Busty Carmel, the three of us will go up to look for him, the constable and I will keep Tully safe."

She looked at me, "then I'm coming with you."

Lyn went to the police car; he used the radio and then returned with a camera and body bag.

"I've contacted the undertaker, and I see no reason for a forensic examination of the corps, still I need a doctor to confirm cause of death. I'll take pictures now. The undertaker and doctor will be here shortly." As Lyn finished photographing my car a fireman came over, he explained that it would be hours before the house could be examined and then only if he pronounced it structurally sound.

I asked Lyn if I could have my car back. I wanted to stop any speculation on what may be found inside the house. He nodded as he photographed the body. "You might want to brush the glass off the seats before you get in."

I managed to stand without help. Carmel watched anxiously she told me I would definitely have concussion and shouldn't stand or turn quickly. I walked towards her; she clapped like a little girl. I hugged her and said. "See how tough I am." She maintained the hug. "Do you know if a hug lasts longer than thirty seconds, your body will release chemicals to make you feel good and prepare you for reproduction?"

"Reproduction, really?"

She smiled and lowered her eyelids, "sex."

I hugged tighter, "Ah, keep hugging, reproduction preparation is happening."

She kissed my ear, "you don't have to tell me, I can feel what's happening and two policemen are watching," We reluctantly drew apart.

"I'm going to brush the seats." I went to the car boot and dragged out a pair of garden gloves and a dust brush. They all looked at me. "What! I like to keep my car clean."

"Give me the brush," Carmel said, "I'll clean the seats, we can vacuum properly when we get home."

I leant on the car as she brushed pebbles of glass from the seats. Lyn was amused, "you want to give the police car a good brushing too?"

He was ignored. The undertaker arrived, quickly followed by the doctor. He squatted beside Walker's corps. "Somebody shot him."

"We believe that's what happened, yep." Lyn nodded, "Do we need an autopsy?"

The doctor rolled the body over, "no, bury him as soon as the next of kin want."

CHAPTER 17

Carmel and I sat in my car. She put her hand on my shoulder. "How long have we known each other Tully?"

I was surprised when I thought about it. "A few days honey. Can I call you honey?"

"I'd prefer if you didn't, but if you really need to, OK"

"Carmel, you make me smile and it hasn't been long but I feel as if we've spent our lives together."

She squeezed my shoulder, "That's just the way I feel, I like it, and I want it to last forever and you can call me darling." She let go of my shoulder, reached over to the back seat and grabbed her handbag. "I kept this." She showed me the revolver, "If there's anything, any danger, I'll use this gun. I don't care if I go to jail."

"It won't come to that, If Busty is still alive, he'll have everything under control, if he's not alive, then the cops can handle it."

We waited; finally, I told Lyn we were going to find Busty. He frowned but nodded, "I won't be long mate. You take care."

We drove slowly up the green ridge; it was wet and slippery as it always is. The GT's tyres were not meant for a slippery track, nor was the growling V8 motor. Whenever the rear end slewed, I heard a gasp from Carmel. I stopped on a slightly more level section of the track.

"I can't go any higher, it's too risky. This is the only place we can turn around without sliding down into the creek. It's still ten minutes' walk to the Caterpillar and the footprint. Do you like walking?"

"Sometimes, today, walking with you will be good."

We climbed over a hump on the ridge; on our right was what Roxanne's girls called 'the slidy track'. The thought of Stella and Bobby caused a terrible sadness. Carmel noticed and stopped walking. A mist was coming in along with light rain.

"What's wrong Tully? Why the tears in your eyes?"

"This is where the little girls came up, not far up the ridge is the Waterfall where Stella fell. It's horrible Carmel, I don't want to think about it, but I can't help it."

She put her arms around me and kissed me. "It's such a sad, sad thing, I wish I could help.

We kept walking; my little D2 came into view. Busty was sitting on the ground leaning on the Caterpillar's tracks. We hurried towards him.

"Can you see anyone around? I asked Carmel.

"No, but he doesn't look right, there's something wrong with him."

We walked up and sat beside him. "Mate, are you OK?" He looked at his hands, both were smeared with blood.

"I'm not OK; I'll never be OK again."

Carmel asked where the blood came from. He showed us his back. She covered her mouth,

"God, they shot you." His back was covered in blood.

"I was a fool; I went to sleep. That little cop Walker grabbed my gun before I could stop him. He shot me as I stood up."

"You've been up here all day wounded and bleeding?"

He looked at me, "When I get my hands on him, I'll break his back and watch him die."

"He's dead mate. Carmel shot his head off."

"I'd rather it was me but good on you, I'm happy." He staggered as he tried to stand.

I told him to sit down and rest, we'd get him to hospital. Carmel would give him an injection.

"I'll never sit down again in my life."

Carmel was looking into the footprint, "Tully I can hear noises from over there."

I was alarmed, "Busty, Ross and his thug could've come up here. I'll look around."

"No, you don't have to; the two of them are up there."

I saw Carmel's hand go into her bag. I shook my head; she kept her hand in the bag.

"Aren't you worried?"

"They're not going anywhere, they can't walk, I fixed the bastards."

"What happened?" Carmel asked.

"I just waited, I knew I couldn't walk down, I knew I'd bleed to death if I moved too much. Then I remembered Tully's father hated snakes. Old Dublin Jack, like all Irishmen he was scared of snakes." He took several deep breaths. "I checked the special tool draw under the Caterpillar's seat. Dublin's double barrel, twenty-gauge, snake gun was always in that draw. He had it cut down to his own measurements, smaller than the cops allow."

I nodded, it was a nasty vicious little thing, and I always kept it maintained and in the draw where Dad had it.

Busty stopped to breathe again. I thought he was going fall over, then he straightened and went on. "I sat over in the trees with the gun beside me covered in grass. They came; they stood in front of me and told me what they'd done to Rocky and my little girls. Ross laughed when he said they'd shot their legs so they couldn't escape the fire. I lifted Dublin's gun out of the grass. A close range twenty gauge in each of their knees."

CHAPTER 18

The mist was closing in on both sides of the ridge. Soon it seemed we were in the only place left in the world.

"What do you want us to do mate?" I asked.

"Right now, Tully there isn't anything you can do," after a long pause he went on," They told me that it was uncle Joe that ordered this punishment. I didn't believe he was a vindictive man now I know different. Trouble is I won't be alive to do anything to him. I'm not asking you to take care of him you understand Tully?"

I nodded, I knew I would.

He looked at us, "When I've rested for a while I'll take care of those two up there and Tully

I'll say goodbye, This, isn't a world I can face anymore."

Carmel was gently crying which upset me greatly, "What will you do now?" She asked.

"I'll take care of the scum waiting up there like I said. I'll just let them suffer a bit longer. You take Tully home and love him. The world will be a better place tomorrow."

I rang Al that night and asked if he and his uncle could go up with me to the falls after lunch tomorrow. He said they would. Lyn called to say he was sorry he didn't get up to the footprint and was Busty OK? I told him we didn't see Busty and didn't know where he was.

Carmel cooked a meal. We sat together on the veranda, and I held her whenever she cried. I knew what would happen after we left Busty. I knew Ross and his mate would now be down in the gorge under the falls. I knew I would never see Busty again.

"Tully, I need to go back to Sydney, I'll have to resign from the practice I was working at, I can't just ring them and tell them I quit. They're nice people and I liked working with them.

I also need to spend some time, a week maybe, with my mother and grandmother, I have a lot to tell them."

I didn't expect this news, I don't know why, I suppose I was thinking I was her life now.

"Of course, Carmel, I'm sorry, of course there must be a lot of things you need to do. When will you go back?"

"As soon as I can, I'll ring the practice tonight, then I'll contact Mom, I want to tell her all about you."

"Will you tell her you're in love?"

"I think that's the first thing I'll tell her, and I know they will definitely want to meet you."

I smiled, "should I be nervous?"

She laughed, "you definitely should be nervous, Betty, my grandmother is a very tough lady and can judge people's character very well, Mom will be apprehensive, my parents haven't had a loving relationship. My father is a politician in the Legislative Council and lives in Sydney, Mom and Bety live in Moss Vale and probably haven't seen him since my graduation."

I told her it would be fine, and I was now looking forward to the meeting.

Al and his uncle arrived. I didn't want to go up to the footprint, but it needed to be done,

Even if just for Al's sake. He was entitled to know the end. I was certain I knew, and I hoped it wouldn't haunt me.

Carmel didn't want to be part of that end story. She decided she would stay and clean my house. We hugged before I left, and I called her a good housewife. She laughed.

Al and his uncle read what they could from the tracks, they often looked at each other. After an hour we came out onto the top of the falls.

"Busty shot both of them, probably in the legs because they fell close to each other." Al's uncle said, "he left them to bleed for a long time, then he dragged them up to the lip of the falls, one at a time and threw them over."

I said nothing, I knew he would do that, wounded as he was.

"You know what's next don't you Tully?"

I couldn't answer.

"He threw himself over actually dragged himself over."

"Busty told me his uncle was responsible for everything they did here." I said, "I wouldn't have believed the old bastard was that vindictive, how could he have thought that murdering his family was going to make the situation better. He told me when I was in Sydney that he would kill Busty."

"What will you do?" Al asked.

I told him I didn't know I'd had enough. couldn't even think straight.

"If you don't finish it, I will." Al said. "Busty would always fight my battles with me. I was welcome in his home, no matter how bad the troubles were that I bought with me. Now there is nothing left. His family horribly murdered."

I knew what he was saying. I couldn't believe what had happened.

"I'm going down to Sydney, I'll shove Joe Castorana 's face in what he's done. I'll make him understand that I'm going to kill him for it."

"I'm sorry Al, you do what you have to do, and I won't be sorry whatever happens to Castorana, but I can't be with you. I need to start a new life with Carmel. I just want to forget." I gave him

Carmel's address in Moss Vale and asked him to come and talk to us before he did anything. I said we would tell her mother and grandmother the whole story. They would know what Carmel did, was forced to do in defending her own life and mine.

He was silent for long minutes, finally he nodded, agreeing to come to Moss Vale.

"Whatever happens, Giuseppe Castorana will not go on living," he vowed.

CHAPTER 19

Carmel was waiting when I arrived home. She had booked her flight to Sydney for the next day, and would hire a car to drive out to Moss Vale.

"Al is going to Sydney; he wants to finish it and lay the ghosts to rest. Carmel, I know he's going to kill Joe Castorana, he's desperate to do this and he'll do it if I'm with him or not."

"He wants me with him. He seems to need to demonstrate to me that he has avenged Busty and Roxanne."

Carmel looked at me wide eyed, searchingly, "Do you have to do this? Do you want to be there?"

"I don't want to live with what has happened already, I don't want to be there, Al and I have been best friends since school, and we've lost Busty and Roxanne for ever. I know what he's feeling."

I looked at her and felt nothing but love, "I'm going with you."

She smiled through tears, "I've booked two seats."

"Because of me you've witnessed all these horrors, you've killed a man."

"Oh, Tully, It's not your fault. I'll never forget what's happened, but I know I can live with the memories."

I hugged her. My life had changed forever. I'd lost my best friend, I'd lost Roxanne. I found the person I wanted to spend my life with, Now I felt tears in my eyes.

"It wasn't you Tully, you didn't open Pandora's box, you tried to help your friends. Now, the last thing out of the box is hope. With hope, together we can build a life with each other forever."

I knew she was serious, I knew I would try, as I've never tried before, and we would build that life together.

"I'll meet your mother and grandmother, even if they hate me and tell me to leave you alone and go back to the bush, I'll still like them."

We were sitting on Carmel's mother's veranda when Al arrived. He hugged each of us in turn, and began speaking.

"This is not only my voice. Ancestors over thousands of years are speaking through me.

Someone has murdered my friends. Friends who treated me as family, who always, from childhood, supported my decisions and dreams, fought my battles with me and openly loved me. Elders from my family say this murderer cannot be left to live his life."

Carmel squeezed my hand. Her mother and grandmother were watching Al.

"You're my people," Al continued, "through Carmel and Tully you're now my people and I would ask for your approval and support."

Carmel's mother held up her hands, palms out, "Albert we know what happened, we listened to the horrifying story Carmel and Tully told, that one man's selfish greed could lead to such tragedy is almost beyond our comprehension, I'll make a cup of tea while we consider what's been said."

I hugged Carmel.

"Leave her alone boy," Betty instructed, "she's beside you now and she'll be beside you for the rest of your life no matter what I say."

I was chastised and put in my place. Carmel squeezed my hand tighter, smiled and stifled a giggle. Betty looked at her and frowned. There was a clash of ebony eyes. Carmel was respectful but not intimidated.

Betty looked at Al, "Mr. Harvey, I accept you as a member of my people and my family."

The tea was brought out, we settled comfortably. I was amazed to see Betty produce a cigarette and light it. "This isn't a democracy," she said, "as has been our way for thousands of years, my daughter and granddaughter can voice their opinions, and they will be considered." We all nodded. She looked at Carmel and her mother, she ignored me.

Carmel's mother said straight out that she believed Castorana must die. With tears in her eyes Carmel agreed.

Betty went on, "We don't have any fighting men left, we don't have what you might call medicine men who can kill from a distance, with magic, but Giuseppe Castorana tried to murder Carmel and was responsible for the awful deaths and horrors committed against your friends. We will support your actions."

Al stood, looked at each of us in turn, "Thank you." He shook my hand and left.

"The punishment will be carried out," Betty said, she addressed herself to Carmel.

"My granddaughter, you need no longer be afraid of what this devil of a man will do to you."

Next night's news carried a report of a well-known Sydney hotel owner falling to his death from the second-floor balcony of his hotel.

Carmel came into my room that night and slid into bed with me. She said we should build a house on top of the highest mountain; we could lie in bed, watch the snow, and forget sadness. I did not have the heart to tell her the snow would never fall in North Queensland.

She said, "hold me Tully, love me tonight, love me forever".